Winter Journey

BOOKS BY ISABEL COLEGATE

The Blackmailer

A Man of Power

The Great Occasion

Statues in a Garden

Orlando King

Orlando at the Brazen Threshold

Agatha

News from the City of the Sun

The Shooting Party

A Glimpse of Sion's Glory

Deceits of Time

The Summer of the Royal Visit

Winter Journey

Isabel Colegate

Winter Journey

COUNTERPOINT

WASHINGTON, D.C.

First U.S. edition published in 2001 by Counterpoint

First published in Great Britain in 1995 by Hamish Hamilton,
a division of Penguin Books Ltd.

Library of Congress Cataloging-in-Publication Data
Colegate, Isabel.
Winter journey / Isabel Colegate.
p.   cm.
ISBN 1-58243-122-1 (alk. paper)
1. Brothers and sisters – Fiction. 2. Middle aged persons –
Fiction. 3. Sibling rivalry – Fiction. 4. Photographers – Fiction.
5. Farm life – Fiction. 6. England – Fiction. I. Title.
PR6053.O414 W56 2001
823'.914 – dc21   00-064449

Printed in the United States of America on acid-free
paper that meets the American National Standards Institute
Z39-48 Standard.

COUNTERPOINT
P.O. Box 65793
Washington, DC 20035-5793

Counterpoint is a member of the Perseus Books Group.

Winter Journey

I

Having travelled, Alfred now lived where he had spent his childhood. The house, the nearby farm buildings, the wood beside, the valley behind, were all to him like consciousness itself, much deeper than appearance. Even when he had been away for several years and had come back, he had not seen them as separate from himself. They were his essence, as the high grassland into which the valley narrowly reached was the essence of the Mendip hares who frequented it. The photographs which filled the attic rooms at the top of the house bore witness to the close scrutiny to which he had subjected his relationship with the place, as well as to his occasionally desperate attempts to escape it. He had overlaid its soft English contours with the drama of the Apennines, imposed on its green watery light the high lucidity of the Himalayas, the black on white shadow of summer in a Mediterranean side street, the dry red rock of a cave in the Atlas mountains. In one of the rooms a woman danced, and jumped into the air, and perhaps flew.

The house sits with its back to the hill, and the land looks as if it rises uniformly behind it towards the higher ground, but in fact the woods to the right of the house conceal a declivity, which is reached by walking across a field, usually full of grazing sheep, and climbing the fence into the belt of tall beeches beyond which the ground unexpectedly slopes down to where the valley, half wood and half pasture and watered by a small fast-flowing stream, inserts itself between the hills, leading nowhere in particular and having therefore no road nor even much of a path. Access being difficult and the slopes steep for ploughing, the fields here have never been anything but pasture, and of late years not much used even for that; wild flowers grow in profusion as a result. Between Christmas 1992 and the early part of the following January the temperature never rose above freezing. There was hardly any wind, and on the days when the freezing fog failed to lift at all there seemed hardly any light either. These muted, motionless days were interspersed with others, motionless too, but sunlit, the distances clear, the shadows long and dark. Even then the ground was frozen hard, the still branches of the trees were white with frost and the ice remained on the puddles on the path through the wood and on the edges of the little stream. Alfred, looking through the lens of a camera, could see the world on another scale; he could track a torrent through a wild valley in the far Pamirs, where the dark current ran thin between frozen shallows and forced its way through huge rocks out on to the valley floor where bears might fish or eagles hunt. When his half-breed collie hopped the stream and spoiled the illusion, he widened his view to show only a quiet field or two among much milder hills, already, though only mid-afternoon, obscured by the returning fog.

Edith, reaching the familiar stretch of straight Roman road off which she had to turn to reach her brother's house (which was also the house in which she herself had grown up) was thankful to have left London in such good time; she would be there before the fog closed in. She had turned the volume of her car radio down because the baritone had been singing some settings of A.E. Housman which she thought were too sentimental, but hoping they were finished by now she turned it up again to hear the quiet opening chords of her father's setting of John Drinkwater's poem about fallow deer.

'Shy in their herding dwell the fallow deer,' sang the baritone, calm above the piano's agitations.

Edith thought how odd it was that after all these years she could still be made to blush by her father. It was ridiculous; and also, when she came to think of it, it was not her father who embarrassed her, so much as herself when young. She had been so keen, and probably rather fat, standing up in front of the whole school, singing Thomas Arne's 'Where the bee sucks'. And how she had shouted in the choir, his favourite child, belting out the choruses as he furiously waved his arms. 'Raise the roof!' he would mouth at them as the fortissimos approached, 'Raise the roof!' in draughty churches and village halls, keeping people's spirits up in the war. There had been one of the Elgar Pomp and Circumstance marches with words put to it, 'Sing then, brother, sing,/Giving everything . . .' Had it been some sort of pageant? She had been dressed up, she was sure of that. Or was she muddling it with the time she had written a play about German spies and they had produced it in the Third Form and there had been a lot of smoke and battles and she had worn Jane Smiley's riding breeches which were rather too small and a tin hat borrowed from one of the air-raid wardens? The parents had laughed so much they had had to repeat it the following night for the ones who had missed it.

> '. . . The fallow deer keep
> Delicate and far their counsels wild.'

He could do a long flexible line of melody; she had always liked that.

> 'Lightfoot, and swift, and unfamiliar,
> These you may not hinder, unconfined
> Beautiful flocks of the mind.'

Yes, well, not so bad, she thought, everyone's of their own time, aren't they? What else can we be?

'"Merrily merrily shall I live now",' she sang loudly, '"under the blossom that hangs on the bough".'

She had sung in the Bach Choir in London for a time, when she was first married, but that was a long time ago; quite different activities had taken over. Perhaps it was a pity.

She slowed down as she approached the turning, partly out of caution because of the icy road and partly because she was not much looking forward to seeing her brother. She expected to find the house a mess and Alfred annoying; at the same time, with Alfred as with her father, nothing was ever as simple as it seemed. Before she came to the turning, a big brown hare suddenly emerged from the hedge beside the road and ran unhurriedly in front of the car for a few yards before loping through a gateway into a field. There had always been hares on the Mendips, though one tended not to see them so much in the winter, and the sight gave her a familiar pleasure.

'A fine Jack hare,' she said aloud.

That reminded her, because she had just been thinking about his music, of the canon her father had composed for the school choir. 'Jack be nimble, Jack be quick, Jack jump over the candlestick.' On and on it would go, at each 'Jack' a new group joining the song, and the whole thing getting faster and faster until the supposedly unanimous if breathless ending. The tune had a jauntiness she had loved at ten, been maddened by at thirteen.

She turned off the road through tall stone pillars and immediately the ice scrunched on the puddles in the rutted drive. The pillars marked the entrance to a vanished house, whose few remaining stones, overgrown by grass and brambles, lay scattered beyond the tumbledown farmyard where the farmer on whose fields it abutted kept a tractor and failed to mend the roof. The old drive led along the side of a copse of hazel; then on the left, before the farmyard, another track turned down to the plain stone farmhouse, embellished only by a shell-shaped hood of stone over the front door, which Arthur Ashby, talented son of a shoemaker from nearby Street, had bought in the late nineteen-twenties on his marriage to the gently born Janet.

Before Edith came in sight of the house, while she was still bumping slowly along the track with the wood on one side and a hawthorn hedge with a field beyond it on the other, all white with frost, she saw a figure emerging from behind the

4

farm buildings ahead, and with her immediate recognition came familiar emotions, quick pleasure and almost as instant irritation. Such a useless thin jacket, he must be frozen; and of course no gloves, because what was the use of gloves when you might need your fingers for something, like taking a photograph? She had knitted him mittens once; he'd never worn them. That was not strictly true; it had been in the war when everyone was supposed to knit for the troops and though at eleven she hated knitting and was not at all good at it, she had wrestled with four needles to produce some misshapen mittens in air-force-blue wool, one pair of which had been rejected on account of the number of dropped stitches. It was these which in turn the eight-year-old Alfred had despised.

He walked unevenly through the frozen mud towards her, followed by what seemed to be even more dogs than usual.

'How lank you look,' she said as he got into the car.

'No lanker than usual surely,' he said, pushing out an eager mongrel and banging the door.

'No. How are you?'

'Very well. You've done well to get here so early.'

He shouted at the dogs, who were jumping up at Edith's new car, doing no good to the paintwork. Edith accelerated and they ran beside, too close, too cheerful.

'Lucky for them I didn't bring my fierce cat.'

'Luckier cat, I'd say.'

At the end furthest from the house the valley narrows into a wood, the stream here busier than lower down, tumbling over a series of miniature waterfalls between the overhanging trees. The path beside the stream leads through the unkempt mixture of ash and hazel, sycamore and thorn, up on to the grassland of the western Mendips, which is patterned by low stone walls and grazed by sheep.

Emerging from the trees and leaving the stream to their right, Edith and Alfred turned towards silence, their horizon limited by mist.

'It's so different, in this weather,' said Edith. 'No huge sky. No larks. No sheep.'

'You haven't been for a bit.'

'It was the summer before last. Or was there a weekend since then? I think there was.'

'It was summer when you came with Sarah and the children.'

'The children loved it. I must bring them again some time. I quite often have them on my own now, it's more fun.'

She had insisted on going for a walk, saying she needed it after sitting in the car for so long. It was what she usually did as soon as she arrived, and Alfred was glad enough to call the dogs and go with her, talking as they went. Her foreign students, her daughter Sarah, local news, mutual friends. Not yet her journalist friend Hubert, or what exactly it was that Alfred did with himself all day, or anything at all to do with money. They were pleased to see each other, and had no wish to explore areas of controversy. Alfred as usual found Edith's confident presence heartening; he was pleased to see how well she looked, striding beside him pink-cheeked in the cold, the grey of her thick curly hair tactfully blended with the still bright brown (at some expense – Edith's natural look had not been achieved through all her adult years without considerable attention to detail). Edith tended to remember how annoying Alfred was until she saw him, when she remembered also how much he amused and surprised her. There he was, in his tattered old coat, without his gloves, needing a shave, nothing to be proud of, and yet she was proud of him; she always had been. If only that wretched woman had not done that awful thing.

'We ought to turn back,' she said.

At the same moment there was a sound of snarling from beyond the nearby wall, followed by one sharp bark and an outburst of high-pitched yapping.

A woman screamed, 'Get off, you brute! Go away!'

A man's voice made incoherent masterful sounds, and the woman said indignantly, 'Poor Dilly!'

6

Alfred called his dogs and they scrambled at once over the wall, being more obedient than their riff-raff appearance suggested. Out of the mist two figures appeared the other side of the wall, indicative of hostility.

'You ought to keep that dog on a lead,' said the woman.

'He doesn't mean it, he's got no teeth,' said Alfred. 'Oh, hullo, Hermione, I didn't see it was you.'

'They looked like teeth to me. Oh, Edith as well, how lovely. How can we get across this wall? Look, Johnny, it's Edith.'

'I know it's Edith. How are you, Edith? God, it's cold. What are we all doing up here?' He wore a riding mackintosh and had a large round red face, lightly moustached and surmounted by a brown felt hat.

'There's a gate along here,' shouted Hermione. She was dressed in much the same way as her husband, but with a Paisley-patterned scarf round her head; her face was as red but more heavily veined so that the cheeks looked purple. She still carried one of her two miniature schnauzers, the other meanwhile bouncing provocatively up to Alfred's dogs.

'Dally!' she shouted unavailingly. 'We're trying to walk off our lunch, we had a whole lot of ghoulish neighbours. You should have come.'

'I thought you'd gone,' Edith said to Johnny. 'Sarah told me you'd sold the house.'

'She was dead right, we have,' said Hermione. 'There's a sale in a week or two, most of the furniture and stuff, Sotheby's are doing it. You ought to come. Not that there'll be any bargains, we hope, but there might be a few old lawn-mowers or something.'

'I'm sorry,' said Edith to Johnny.

'It's not too bad,' he said.

'We were terrified of not finding a buyer,' said Hermione. 'Bloody Lloyd's has done for so many other people as well as us, we thought there might be no one to buy it. Masses of people came round though, pop stars and so on mainly. They all wanted to know where they could put their recording studios. Of course they were frightfully put off when they realized there wasn't a swimming pool.'

'Did a pop star buy it?' asked Alfred.

'No, a lawyer from Hong Kong. He wants to put in a golf course.'

'We're renting a little house on the Quantocks,' said Johnny. 'She wants to breed schnauzers. They're getting very popular now. I might do a bit of fishing.'

'You'll miss it,' said Edith.

'No alternative,' he said. 'The children are going to have to manage. Sarah's all right with her business and that banker husband. Bit pompous I find him, don't you?'

'I know what you mean, but I've got quite fond of him. What about your boys?'

'Army, nature films and ski-bum,' said Hermione. 'They're fine. Come and see us before Edith goes back, I'll give you a ring. Come on, Johnny, we'll be lost in the dark if we don't go home.'

Alfred suggested they came to tea and let him drive them home but they refused politely and stumped off into the mist.

'What a nightmare,' said Edith.

'Selling Thorngrave?'

'That perhaps. But I really meant her.'

'Sarah says she's very kind.'

'Oh yes and sporting and generally agreed to be a jolly good sort. Poor Johnny, he really doesn't deserve it.'

'Perhaps you should have thought of that when you left him.'

'He was so agonizingly boring.'

'Of course. But you must have once thought he wasn't.'

'I only married him to please Mummy.'

'Oh, Edith, you never did anything to please Mummy.'

'To get away from her, then.'

'All I can say is, he was always very nice to me, poor old Johnny. Getting me a job and so on.'

'All you did was go to sleep in an armchair in that awful coffee place in the City.'

'I liked it, Bunty's it was called, you could play chess as well as going to sleep. Besides, that wasn't his fault, it was mine. I'm very sorry he's lost all his money. They've been there for generations, his family.'

'He's too stupid to mind.'

'Being stupid wouldn't stop him minding. Rather the opposite, I'd have thought. And it will be funny to have all these Chinese people playing golf all over the place.'

'I don't suppose he's Chinese, the Hong Kong lawyer.'

'Don't you think so?'

'They mostly aren't, if they come to settle here. It's just that that's where they've made their money.'

'I see. I quite thought he would be Chinese. I think we should ring up Johnny, just to be sure.'

2

The house, four-square and sober, was distinguished by its staircase, and the fact that it had three storeys. The staircase was of oak and its heavy bannisters were unexpectedly baroque, suggesting a grander past than the rest of the house lived up to. The big house to which the drive had once led, curving to bypass the farm buildings, had been built in the eighteen-thirties and partly demolished in the nineteen-thirties, when the coal-owning family who lived there had fallen on hard times and there were no buyers to be found in those recession-ary years. The farmhouse was a much earlier building and might have been part of a former estate centred round a house which had preceded, or been engulfed by, the nineteenth-century building. This would have accounted for the staircase and the fine stonework of the farmhouse, which might have been built for a son of the big house, or housed a widow. Mr and Mrs Sainty, local historians who were new acquaintances of Alfred's, knew some of the history of the place, but most was lost in obscurity.

At the top of the staircase was a large, light landing. There were two bedrooms at the front of the house, two at the back. Edith, who after her parents' death and during the period of her second marriage had spent much time at the house, had taken over what had been her parents' big front bedroom, but Alfred still slept in the room which had always been his, at the back of the house looking out towards the hills. A door just outside his room led to the narrow back stairs and the top floor, the whole of which he had gradually appropriated, spreading out from the bathroom, which he had turned into his darkroom, and filling all the available space with a miscellany of apparatus and images. It was rare these days for anyone other than Alfred to go up those stairs.

Alfred's bedroom was seldom tidy, but its confusion was decorative, largely because of all the things he had brought back from his travels – rugs, cushions, lengths of fabric he had never decided what to do with so left draped about at random, boxes, scarves, carvings, odd lumps of lapis lazuli or amethyst. The books in the shelves, surprisingly perhaps, were neatly arranged in subject order. At night he liked reading heavy biographies of unpleasant men. Dictators, swindlers, Mafia bosses, Presidents of the United States, newspaper tycoons, passed before his mild eyes and sent him comfortably to sleep. Not always, though. On the first night of Edith's visit, propped on his pillows with the latest life of Lord Beaverbrook resting against his knees, he felt an unaccountable restlessness. His attention wandered, flickering anxiously around Edith, their encounter in the fog, the suddenly alerted part of his memory in which Johnny was younger and Edith was his wife, their parents alive, he himself in what he still looked on as total ignorance of everything because he had not yet met Lydia; all this accumulated into an extreme agitation. He closed the book. He remembered how once in a rest house in Sikkim he had passed a night in anguished distress quite unrelated to the untroubled mood in which he had arrived at the place, only to find in the morning that an Australian hippy sleeping at the other end of the building had killed himself during the night with an overdose of heroin. When one's mind had loosed its anchor, ready to dream, it was open to invasion; these must be Edith's anxieties, not his. He put on an old Afghan coat which smelt faintly of goat, a pair of socks and some espadrilles, because the central heating went off at night, and went quietly out of his room and up the back stairs.

The darkroom smelt as usual of the chemicals he used for developing; in the dim, red light of the specially darkened bulb he moved the trays, poured out the necessary liquids, dipped the first negative and waited for the image to emerge: Winter, 1992–3, the valley transformed by frost.

Edith sometimes claimed to be all in favour of anxiety. 'Where would I be if I didn't worry?' she would say when people adjured her to be calm. 'Worry keeps me going.' She thought she knew how to control it, kept lists, and accounts, and a most efficient filing system. If ever she found herself sleepless she made a cup of tea, read a book, brushed her hair, firmly told herself an adventurous tale in which her own role was highly creditable. On a night so cold as this, however, she was unwilling to leave her warm bed to go down to the kitchen, where the dogs slept and might wake and bark and disturb Alfred, and no heroic tale could convince her when she was possessed by self-reproach.

She might say she believed in worrying about the future, but she had never approved of regrets about the past. When she felt she had made a mistake, she tried to learn from it, indeed she could nag away in her mind at some small incident, a misunderstanding at a meeting, a sudden realization that someone she had been dealing with had not responded to her friendliness (seeing it, possibly rightly, as designed to secure her own ends), until she felt she had understood its significance and decided whether the situation could be redeemed; but where something had gone wrong through no fault of hers, or where the fault was hers but was irreparable, she bore no malice and made no reproaches, even to herself. She had sacked people, where she considered it necessary, without a qualm, first in her play-group organization, then in her political office, and now occasionally in her language school; she did not suffer much from doubts, and since what she did she did because she thought it right, there seemed no point in undermining the whole endeavour by beginning to think it might be wrong. That could only lead to indecision, the worst of weaknesses.

In the cold bedroom, once her parents', all this common

sense and competence for the moment failed her; it was not an adequate defence against what the freezing fog had so unexpectedly disclosed, against the pity, and consequently the shame, which Alfred's casual remarks had loosed in her, or against the questions, long familiar and long avoided, for which the silence of the darkened house, broken only by the occasional unaccountable creaking as of a wooden ship in a calm sea, seemed to leave a quite disconcerting amount of space.

Alfred had said, 'Being stupid wouldn't stop him minding. Rather the opposite, I'd have thought.'

It was true that Johnny had always had a way of holding out his hurt feelings like a dog with a sore paw, reproachful and uncomprehending.

'But you're so stupid, Johnny, you don't understand anything. Don't you see I'm just dying of boredom?'

You had to be very young to be as unkind as that. Had she never been kind to him? She must have cheered him up a bit, presumably, at one time, ordering him about, laughing at him, giving him an occasional hug. He had been so keen to please in bed, asking if she'd liked it, whether he was any good. How was she to know? She'd never done it before: she thought the fact that she preferred just kissing to the actual consummation was something to do with her own inexperience and did not tell him, because the actual consummation seemed to mean so much to him. Perhaps that was kind. Perhaps it was kind to have danced with him so much when they first met, all those foxtrots at Hunt Balls, Tea for Two and Two for Tea, and then the Post Horn Gallop at the end. Johnny was a neat dancer, correct and rhythmical, often humming the tune. Whenever there was a waltz he would appear at her side, only slightly sweaty and smiling happily; he was sweatier by the end of the waltz but she did not mind because she was exalted. Once they danced a polka. It was rare for the band to play a polka; even the waltz only came up once or twice in an evening; but there they were in

London in the Hyde Park Hotel, dancing a polka. Edith was eighteen. Her mother had said, 'How nice of the Cornishes to ask you, they really didn't need to.'

Caroline Cornish had been a schoolfriend; she was a proper débutante, not a mere hanger-on at the fringes like Edith. She had been to a Buckingham Palace garden party and Queen Charlotte's Ball and a dance or two every night, in London on weekdays and all over the country at weekends. 'So amazing that it's all come back,' said Edith's mother. 'Of course it's not like before the war, but you wouldn't think people could afford it at all with taxation at eighteen shillings in the pound.' She renewed some of her old acquaintance, for Edith's sake – 'One rather lost touch with people in the war' – spent money on clothes for herself as well as for Edith, and in her quiet way enjoyed it. 'So lovely to feel one's celebrating a return to normal.' Edith proclaimed the whole thing to be perfectly ridiculous, a waste of time, a snobbish farce, and appealed to her father.

'Nonsense, Edie, of course you must have some fun at your age. You don't have to start your singing until September.'

'But the men are completely stuffed, you've never seen such things.'

He frowned, ready to be protective. 'Don't they ask you to dance?'

'Yes, of course they do.'

'That's all right, then.'

So she danced, often with Johnny, because she knew him already, from Hunt Balls in the country; and at Caroline Cornish's dance at the Hyde Park Hotel they danced a polka.

'I don't know how to,' she said.

'One two three hop,' he said. 'Faster, faster. We'll take diagonals.'

They rushed from one corner of the floor to the other, lesser dancers clearing away on either side like the waters of the Red Sea, one two three hop, one of Johnny's hands clasped to hers and held out before them like the prow of a ship, the other firmly holding her waist, one two three hop, her dress swinging and swirling, dark pink chiffon with darker pink towards the ground, full skirt, tight ruched bodice, strapless. 'Like a flame,' he gasped. 'Your dress. Like a flame.' And they turned and were off again. 'You're wonderful,' he said. 'Wonderful.' When it ended and they were laughing and breathless, people clapped them, laughing too, even the band; she in her pink dress with her thick bright hair and bashful smile.

Edith sat up abruptly in the big comfortable bed, turned on the light, reached for her dressing-gown and put it round her shoulders. She did not want to think about the past. She had bought a new mattress for the bed when she was married to Derek, her second husband; she had had new curtains made at about the same time, when the William Morris designs first came back into circulation some time in the sixties. Now the green willow leaves had turned sear and yellow where the sunlight had struck them. If they were ever to be replaced she would have to organize and pay for the new ones, because Alfred would see no need for change and had less money than she had; but she was fond of the pattern and thought they had several years of wear in them yet. On the other hand the mahogany wardrobe looked starved of polish; she would have a word with Mrs Weeks, tactfully of course, because Mrs Weeks considered that she worked for Alfred and not for Edith and tended to resent Edith's interference. This was on the assumption that Mrs Weeks still came in to clean two or three times a week. If Edith put her new plan into operation, she might have to ask Mrs Weeks and her daughter Mrs Jupp if they would come more often.

Hoping to have dispelled the repetitive polka tunes, Edith put aside her dressing-gown, turned out the light and lay down again, thinking calmly about her plan. Like most of her undertakings it was well worked out, timed, costed and committed to paper. The only doubtful quantity was Alfred, on whose agreement it depended, and lying now awake in Alfred's house, which though she had always shared it emotionally she had not shared legally for many years, she was aware of his continuing capacity to undermine her best-laid plans. What seemed to Edith quite obviously the best thing to do had a way of appearing to Alfred in quite a different light. This had always worried Edith, not so much for her own sake but because as his older sister she had never felt it was in Alfred's best interest that he should see things in a light markedly different from her own.

He had looked like a young heron beside his neat, diminutive mother in the front pew of the village church. 'I shall be quite all right, I shall have Alfred with me,' Janet Ashby had said when her husband had wanted to play the organ for the wedding march. Alfred was their mother's hero, humbly accepting her devotion as essential to his managing to keep his head above water at all, standing there beside her scrubbed but still unkempt, so thin in his adolescence as to verge on concavity, while their father swayed and thundered at the organ, beating the Widor toccata out of its dusty pipes as if he were the west wind at loose over the Atlantic, on whose turbulent surf Edith in cream silk taffeta billowed on Johnny's arm past her mother's tremulous smile, which expressed her hope and apprehension and pride.

Edith turned over, adjusted the pillows; what had Alfred meant by saying that she had never done anything to please her mother? Of course she had married to please her – partly anyway – to satisfy her that her daughter had been accepted back into the world she herself came from, had married into the county, would have in due course the running of a sizable Regency house in which Janet Ashby had played as a child, would have children who would play with the grandchildren of those same childhood companions. All that had meant a great deal to Janet Ashby, and Edith had known that it did. Janet had come back to England from India on her father's retirement in 1929, a spinster in her late thirties, no suitable

army officer or member of the administration having presented himself as a possible husband; she had found life in her
family's home county of Somerset quite uninteresting until,
being musical, she went to help with the choir at the nearby
girls' boarding school and met the dynamic head of the music
department, already locally famous as the composer Arthur
Ashby. Her sweet soprano voice, her gentleness, her extreme
correctness, enchanted the ebullient musician; he thought her
an angel, she responded by thinking him a genius. Their
happy marriage persisted on this understanding, entirely satisfactory to themselves but sometimes irritating to such others
as did not subscribe to its basic tenets. Among those were
their children; Edith did not believe that her mother was an
angel, Alfred that his father was a genius.

Edith turned over again, pulled up the blankets. Now, she
thought, to send myself to sleep I will walk through our first
house, Johnny's and mine, when we were young married
people living in Chelsea in the late fifties, without much
money because Johnny's father believed a young man should
make his own way in the world. I open the blue front door,
and here in the narrow front hall and up the stairs is the *toile
de Jouy* wallpaper with pink shepherdesses on it which I was
so fond of. First I turn left into the sitting-room, which runs
from front to back with a window at each end, pale grey
stripes and curtains with brown and white greyhounds and
blue roses, and the black bookcase Johnny's parents gave us
and the worn Persian rugs which came from my maternal
grandparents, bought by them on the borders of Afghanistan;
then up the stairs, past the bathroom on the half-landing, to
the two bedrooms, one of which became Sarah's, and there's
the health visitor and I'm explaining anxiously about the
nappy-rash, and then downstairs again because our bedroom
door is shut even though Caroline Cornish once said she'd
been in a cinema queue the other side of the road (that was
when there was still that little cinema on the corner) and had
seen me up at the window with nothing on (the film was

Fanfan la Tulipe); and so down past the damp spare room badly built on at the back, where Alfred lodged for a time before he moved into a bedsitting-room somewhere near Victoria, and into the dark little dining-room where we made a mistake over the wallpaper, covering one wall with a dark green geometrical pattern and the others with trailing ivy in a slightly different green, and behind that is the tiny kitchen in which the washing-up seems never to be quite finished and where Johnny and I had an actual fight about how to roast a chicken. Caroline Cornish is perched on a stool in the coffee bar round the corner, and I cross the road to the pawn shop with my engagement ring because Johnny has been playing *chemin de fer* again with his gambling friends and we need to license the Morris Minor, and I pass the antique shop with its three narrow rooms crowded with furniture, and I go in and the friendly owner is there and this I know is on the verge of sleep because there never was such a shop and yet when I dream of these places, which I quite often do, the shop is always there and I am looking for something, but peacefully, there is no anxiety in the search, only it is quite extraordinarily interesting. I think there is a flower shop next to the antique shop. I think that was never there either.

3

'If it wasn't for what I feel I owe her memory I'd have given up coming long ago,' said Mrs Weeks. 'She was always good to me, Mrs Ashby.'

Her daughter, who had heard this before and knew it to be a gross over-simplification of her mother's motives, said nothing, continuing to peer anxiously through the windscreen into the freezing fog, which was made dazzling by a brightness beyond it which hinted at the morning sun. As they turned off the main road, the car lurched into a deep rut; the bottom scraped along the frozen surface of the drive.

'Keep going,' said Mrs Weeks sharply, grabbing the dashboard in front of her with one perfectly manicured hand. 'You'll never get there if you stop the whole time.'

'I'm not stopping,' said her daughter. 'I'm just not used to the car yet. Besides I can't see very well.'

'Nothing new in that. Keep your good eye forward.'

'I always do,' said Mrs Jupp, but her eyes, good and bad, filled with tears.

'No need to start snivelling,' said Mrs Weeks, but she spoke almost absent-mindedly; her daughter's plaintiveness and her own bullying were the conditions of a relationship on which both were equally dependent.

Mrs Weeks patted her silk headscarf and pulled down the passenger mirror to check her lipstick; she picked up the smart red leather handbag from near her feet and held it on her knee, ready to disembark. Edith had given her both the scarf and the handbag at previous Christmases, but Mrs Weeks was not grateful. Gratitude was not an emotion with which she was familiar. Only child of doting parents, she had won the Little Girl Most Like Shirley Temple competition at the local Church fête in 1929, and had had from then on an exaggerated notion as to what was her due. Her husband, a railwayman, had never been allowed to forget his luck in having secured her as his bride, and her daughter Doris (after Doris Day) had been so conscious of her own unworthiness to be the daughter of such a mother that she had apparently married with the idea of securing perpetual punishment; it was not until her brutish husband had beaten her up so badly that she almost lost the sight of one eye that she could be persuaded to leave him and return to her mother, bringing with her her son Sean, usually referred to by his grandmother as 'that boy', to express her deep disapproval of the only person in the neighbourhood she failed to frighten.

She had not frightened Janet Ashby, because in spite of, or perhaps because of, her immense ego, Mrs Weeks was a perfectionist, and during the years she worked for the Ashbys in the fifties she had been a perfect domestic servant. This irritated Arthur Ashby, who complained that Grace, for such was the name she had assumed although she had been christened Gladys, was too deferential by half. In fact he suspected her of laughing at him, because everyone in those parts knew that his father had been a shoemaker, but Janet had explained that it was all because she had been trained under Mr Hood, the butler at the Hall, and that this fact gave her a particular status in her own eyes, so that to have hinted that she was over-playing her part would have been to undermine her self-respect, something that Janet was too kind to consider.

Mrs Weeks had never been deferential to Edith or Alfred, both of whom she had known since they were children, and both of whom she addressed by their first names although they would never have dreamed of calling her anything but Mrs Weeks nor her daughter anything but Mrs Jupp; but after the elder Ashbys' deaths, she had somehow never quite severed the connection, coming back from time to time for a few weeks or months rather as the mood took her, until on Alfred's settling altogether into the place in the mid-eighties

20

she had decided the best thing would be for her to come twice a week, bringing Mrs Jupp 'to do the rough' as she put it, now that she herself was getting older. The arrangement suited Alfred very well; he always made an effort to tidy up the house before they came. They had lately taken to bringing their lunch and spending most of the day there, so that they could do his ironing as well as the cleaning; he gratefully paid whatever Mrs Weeks from time to time told him he owed them. Mrs Weeks's appearance was a source of wonder to him, being such a riot of cosmetic art and such eloquent testimony to the talents of her visiting hair stylist, and he liked to think that Mrs Jupp enjoyed her work; he had more than once seen a faint smile on her asymmetrical face as she ironed his shirts while her mother, scarlet-tipped fingers safely protected by rubber gloves, rewashed the dishes he thought he had left clean the night before and vilified their neighbours.

'That Edith,' said Mrs Weeks, as the car stopped rather abruptly in front of the house. 'Never minds where she puts her car.'

Edith, coming out of the house at that moment, greeted them both and offered to move it. Mrs Jupp assured her that it was not in the least in the way. Edith commented on the good condition of Mrs Jupp's car.

'That boy got it for her,' said Mrs Weeks. 'Where he gets the money I don't know.'

A look of pain crossed Mrs Jupp's face; she did not know either and had been only partially reassured by her son's bland evasions.

Having taken possession of the kitchen, by means of a great deal of bustling about, hanging up of coats, disposing of handbags, rubbing of hands, rearranging of mugs on the dresser (Mrs Weeks preferred them to be hung up in order of size whereas Alfred favoured a more random disposition) and a final filling of the kettle and putting of it in its place on the Aga, Mrs Weeks announced to Mrs Jupp that they would

21

start in the study so that Edith could settle down in there when they had finished, and the two of them moved off with an assortment of equipment, leaving Edith to make herself a cup of Nescafé and sit at the table close to the Aga to read the proposed new brochure for her language school which she had brought with her to revise. From outside came the disagreeably loud noise of Alfred cutting up logs with a motor saw. She had come down for a cup of tea to revive her after her restless night to find him whistling 'See Me Dance the Polka' as he made the toast; disconcerted, she had asked him why, but he did not know and seemed puzzled by her query.

'Have you had any more planning applications?' she asked, to change the subject. 'I always think someone might want to do something with those farm buildings one day.'

'No, no, recession time now. Nice peaceful things, recessions.'

Ten years ago Edith had written to him in India telling him about the planning application to build an artificial ski-slope in the valley and forwarding to him the letter from the company concerned offering him a startlingly large sum of money for a small part of the field behind the house; they needed it in order to build an access road.

'People here are very worked up about it,' she had written. 'It's your property, not mine, so you'll have to decide. Do you want me to send you more details, or might you come back quite soon?'

He had not wanted to think about the valley.

'I went grass-skiing once,' he wrote to Edith. 'Tom Mc-Creery from school knew someone who rented a field to some people who organized it. You did it on sort of huge roller skates. It wasn't much fun, I can't see it catching on. I've written to the people for more details of exactly which part of the field they want.'

It was so dry where he was that it was hard to summon up the memory of the deep green of the valley in summer. He had been living for some weeks in a sand-coloured castle in north-eastern Rajasthan, a succession of arcaded courtyards linked by a confusing network of small stairways and passages, off one of which was the large high room in which he slept. He had a brass bedstead and a hard mattress, a pillared alcove containing a writing table and a defunct but beautifully polished 1930s radiogram, and more mattresses under the three windows with louvred shutters from which when he lay reading he could overlook the wide entrance courtyard, which was bounded by a crumbling castellated wall. From this courtyard, on the occasions (not frequent) when there were other paying guests, the owner Mr Singh, a handsome and jovial ex-army officer who owned many acres of virtual desert, would lead expeditions by car or mini-bus to see the painted havelis of the now decamped merchants and to help out neighbouring land-owners by consuming large meals of wildly varying edibility. Mr Singh, and his beautiful wife and several children, lived mostly in their flat in Delhi and only visited their country estate in the tourist season. The rest of the time the castle was inhabited by his two old aunts, one of whom lived a life so circumscribed by age and ill-health that Alfred hardly ever saw her; the other was an obsessive gardener and was to be found every morning supervising operations in the walled garden on the opposite side of the house from the entrance, where at least six gardeners spent many hours a day sweeping, watering, weeding and gently chattering. Once when Alfred was sitting out there Aunt Parvati said to him, 'They are very idle. You are quite right' – though he had said nothing – 'but you see there is nothing else for them to do. It is better that they sweep leaves here and there in my garden than sit on a wall in one of the towns waiting to be hired as day labourers and then walk all the way home again having earned sweet Fanny Adams for their families.'

She was an expert on the Mughal gardens of India; they used to talk of the book she would write, and the journeys they would make together so that he could take photographs for it, but somehow it was never the right time of year – her nephew was bringing a party without his wife and she would need to organize the kitchen, her sister could not be left, she herself had been having headaches, needed to rest; she continued to discuss their itinerary with animation but he knew their journey would always be deferred.

Every day he drove to another village – there were three hundred or so to choose from – where there were houses with frescoed walls. He had been working for a Japanese travel magazine, whose editor had now commissioned him to provide illustrations for a series of articles by a Japanese expert on the wall-paintings of the merchants' houses of the Shekavarti area. Unsurprised, since he had learned that there was a Japanese expert on everything, he had found out where to go and begun a task which could have lasted for months. All day he crossed the dry land to look at the pictures which the nineteenth-century Marwari merchants had commissioned to amuse their families in this remote part until the caravan routes were made obsolete by the railways and the merchants followed trade to Calcutta, becoming for the most part millionaires as a result. Faded images of Ganesh the elephant god over the entrance, Krishna among the apple trees and the fleeing maidens on dirty courtyard walls, a girlish soldier smelling a rose, a European couple strolling with their umbrellas, miniature towns with peaceful cultivation going on in the fields around them, trotting camels, marching armies, Queen Victoria sitting plumply on a cushion, an elephant caparisoned in gold with Hanuman the monkey god laughing on his back, men and women flying kites, bicycles with tiny wheels, trains with endless different coloured carriages, flowers, trees, birds, gardens, dancing girls, lovers, a holy man, a man going shooting in a top hat, all this on the walls of courtyards now filthy, or under the eaves of houses in which only one room was lived in by a family making candles, or where four or five women worked furiously at ancient sewing machines, or into which a flock of goats was driven in the evening.

When he went back to the castle, he had a bath and lay in his room reading, or wandered through the empty courtyards, or walked in the garden as the moon rose. It might have been possible to defer his return to England indefinitely, just as Aunt Parvati deferred their journey to see the Mughal gardens. The idea attracted him, but there was something in his reading which militated against it, and as well as that the monsoon was late in coming and the toytown images he was recording were beginning to irritate him in the context of so much dryness, such painfully thin cattle. Only where there was a spring, and a patch of irrigated land, would there be meticulous cultivation and welcome green. Otherwise there were only the flocks of scavenging goats, which wandered the dry earth and climbed the stunted bushes in search of leaves.

Walking through a village one day he came to a big baobab tree in the plentiful shade of which was spread a profusion of vegetables. Green beans overflowed their baskets, small potatoes spilled out of sacks, there were glossy plum-coloured aubergines, bunches of feathery green coriander, wicker trays piled high with broad beans, pyramids of small round cabbages. An old man of distinguished appearance and fine white moustaches sat peacefully with his back to the tree while two younger men, one in a bright blue vest, the other in a faded orange shirt, dealt with the customers. On the edge of a piece of sacking on which were heaped young carrots and dark green capsicums a thin girl sat cross-legged, suckling a tiny baby. She was under-nourished, but not tragically so; the baby, as far as Alfred could tell, looked healthy, held tightly in the crook of her arm and sheltered by the fold of the dim shawl which covered her head. He thought afterwards that she might have been a little feverish, perhaps hardly recovered from the birth. The look she gave him was imper-sonal; it was as if he had intercepted a question which was being asked of someone else. But it was asked with such urgency, and her whole countenance was alight with such vivid intelligence, that he turned away, stricken. A minute later he turned back, and bought a shining dark purple aubergine from the man in the blue vest, handing him a note and refusing the change. The girl's head was bent over the child.

He gave the aubergine to the boy who greeted him as he walked into the castle courtyard. 'Catch!' he said, and the boy jumped and caught it with one hand as if it were a cricket ball and then ran off with it, laughing.

Alfred was surprised when a little bowl of brinjal curry was brought to his table that evening; he had meant the boy to keep the aubergine. Dinner was served outside at small tables, dimly lit by candles in jam jars. Next to him was a newly arrived Australian couple. Otherwise there were three German airline stewards who had been there for two days and the two aunts of the proprietor. In anticipation of the tourist season, which never seemed quite to reach its expected peak, an old man with a flaming torch and an embroidered waistcoat performed an unsteady processional dance along the garden path beyond the tables, followed by a sweet-faced girl in a moon–pale sari and a delicately handsome youth in green silk. The youth had a sitar, on which he played a repetitive tune of plangent melancholy, while from time to time the girl produced an unexpectedly loud caterwauling on an apparently unrelated theme. Left vulnerable by the sudden blow to the heart which he had sustained at the vegetable stall, Alfred found himself violently resentful of the Australians' too open amusement. Back in his room he lay on the mattress by the window looking over the moonlit courtyard and felt his own inadequacy before the vastness of the questions India asked. It was not an unfamiliar feeling, nor even an unpleasant one, being for the most part simply melancholy, like the song of the sitar. This time though, he thought he had better go home.

4

The farm buildings were half-concealed from the house by a
huge chestnut tree, which marked the place where the drive
forked. One part of it, now only a track overgrown with
grass, led on past the farmyard towards the site of the ruined
house; the other curved sharply down to the farmhouse. The
farm building, which was Victorian and built of red brick,
had a portentousness lacking in the sunny house to which it
sat at right angles, half concealed by the interposing chestnut
tree. A casual explorer of byways might have thought as he
bumped along the drive that this substantial building was
the only one there, unaware at first of the ruined house
beyond and taken by surprise, as indeed Arthur Ashby had
been when he had first discovered it, by the calm stone façade
of the farmhouse which appeared on his left as he cleared the
wood. Some of the single-storey edifice was now obscured
by ivy, and most of its roof was in obvious need of repair,
but the pointed gable over the central coach-house door still
gave it a certain pretension, as if it might once have been a
schoolhouse rather than a stable. The yard had been cobbled,
with flat square stones which sloped slightly towards a shallow
central runnel leading to a drain, but it was now overgrown
with weeds and in one corner a heap of rubble marked the
place where not long since enterprising thieves had removed
a sizable patch of cobblestones for resale in the local builders'
yard, which had rechristened itself the Architectural Reclama-
tion Centre but was known locally by its old name of Shady
Lane's, its proprietor a Mr Lane being known not to be too
particular as to the provenance of the goods he handled.

Edith approached carefully on the slippery cobbles. The
sun was breaking through the fog but had not melted the

frost. Alfred's dogs preceded her enthusiastically into the
empty loose boxes; one happy autumn had brought migrating
rats, long since exterminated by methods more reliable than
theirs, but they lived in hope. There were pig-sties and two
loose boxes down one side of the three-sided building, a row
of stalls and a former milking parlour in the central section
and a barn on the third side. There was a rusty harrow in the
barn, and a pile of black plastic sacks. Apart from that there
was no sign of use. Edith walked through the building with
increasing excitement, seeing how easily it could be adapted
to her purposes. There was an outside tap, frozen up now of
course but indicating the presence of a water supply. Somewhere inside behind it would be the place for the showers
and lavatories, then there could be a few little separate
bedrooms, a dormitory which would make use of the wooden
stalls to give a certain amount of privacy, a kitchen beyond it
and a dining hall cum lecture room in the barn. There could
be room for up to fifteen students to start with; visiting
lecturers might sometimes have to stay in the house.

Edith stood in the barn, thinking about heating.

> Who said, mum's the word?
> Rust to the harrow

That was another of her father's songs, his slow C minor
setting of Walter de la Mare's poem.

> Who said where lies she now
> Where rests she now her head
> Bathed in eve's loveliness?
> That's what I said

Lydia, thought Edith. Poor Lydia. But then she thought
resentfully how tiresome Lydia had been, thoroughly tiresome
and affected and in the end mad. Standing in the freezing
cold dusty barn, Edith realized how much of her present
reluctance to speak to Alfred about her project was because
of Lydia. When Lydia had been living with Alfred, there had

been horse-drawn caravans in the farmyard and the summer air had been full of pop music and the smell of marijuana. They never talked about Lydia now. Edith was uncertain as to Alfred's buried feelings. Did he associate the farmyard with those days? Was that why when she had asked about it, he had answered so quickly and so apparently casually? She had thought at the time it might have been because he had some other plan for it, or else that he suspected hers and did not like it. She could not expect him to like it. He considered himself a recluse; of course he would not like the idea of twenty-five strange young people invading his house – for she wanted to make use of the house, and indeed of Alfred himself. He could give the students talks on anything he liked, English life, buildings, history, photography, his travels; he would love it once he started. The school would pay him, which would surely be useful; goodness knew how he lived on what he earned from his photography. Only the idea had to be put to him carefully, in the right light. Perhaps it would be wise to emphasize how much she herself needed a new enterprise, how bored she was with the language school now that it was so well established, how much she hoped that if Sarah could be persuaded to take an interest, Sarah's children might benefit from more country air. At the same time she must make it clear that she never for one moment forgot that it was Alfred's house and not hers, and that she could not think of impinging on his independence by buying the farm buildings without his agreement.

Edith walked back to the house, past the chestnut tree. Alfred was still sawing logs.

'I'm going to walk past John Jarrett's,' she shouted above the noise of the saw. 'Will you call the dogs?'

He silenced the saw and whistled to the dogs.

'I've got to go to the village later,' he said. 'Do you want anything?'

'No, but I might come with you if you haven't gone when I come back. I'm only going for half an hour or so while the sun's out. I don't want the dogs, because he always has such a pack of them up there.'

'All quite out of control, too. You know the old man died?'

'Did he? I wondered. When?'

'A year or so ago. Probably before you were last here. There's only young John Jarrett now.'

'He must be over fifty.'

'I heard he was going to sell it but I don't know what happened. I haven't seen him lately.'

Edith took the overgrown track towards the ruined house. The grassy bumps and hollows which were all that remained of the once substantial building were solidly frozen even where the white hoar frost on the grass had melted. When she tried to take a short cut by climbing over one of the miniature mountains familiar to her as a childhood playground, she slipped and almost fell. Reverting to the level ground, she remembered Marjorie, the girl who had looked after her, and how they had stood talking with old John Jarrett's shepherd, a boy called Colin, Edith being then no more than three or four years old. Colin had cut his thumb quite badly; it was wrapped in a bloody handkerchief, not very clean. He had a big clasp knife, might have been peeling an apple. Marjorie rebandaged the wound with a clean handkerchief of her own. Edith was excluded from the pleasure the two of them derived from this procedure, which seemed to take a long time, their heads bent, she murmuring about doctors and disinfectant, he demurring, pleased by her concern. And then a sheep, which had been staring at Edith with mad and haughty eyes, stamped its foot, took a few steps towards her, and shoved her in the stomach with its head. She sat down suddenly with a cry of astonishment. Marjorie turned round, shocked, and hurried to pick her up; Colin – but it was not Colin, she now remembered, it was Tony – Tony kicked the sheep. Marjorie looked back at him as she hurried Edith away, but he was whistling to his dog and did not see. Edith remembered clearly her own intense

30

humiliation; to be knocked down by a sheep! She was fond of Marjorie, but Marjorie was not her equal; nor was Tony, who had an outside man's roughness and smell. What Edith minded was to have lost face; it was her pride which was hurt. Kind Marjorie must have understood, because she ceased reviling the offending sheep, and changed the subject; Edith remembered her own gratitude though even that was shaming. Marjorie and Tony must be old by now, if they were still alive, and John Jarrett had been succeeded by young John Jarrett, who she supposed had gone down in the world rather than up but was not at all deferential. In that respect of course things had changed for the better; Edith was a little priggish in her attitude towards class distinctions, and thought about them more than was quite consonant with her frequently expressed belief that they had ceased to exist.

She crossed two fields and climbed a gate into a small lane. The going was easier here because the ice had thawed where cars had been along the road. Edith walked briskly until she came to two tall stone gateposts, much like the ones which stood at the entrance to the house she still thought of as 'ours' rather than 'Alfred's'; in this case, however, a plain wrought-iron gate hung between them, and was closed. Edith hesitated. The gateposts were new, and so was the gate, but they looked as if they might have been there for years; someone, with a good deal of both money and discrimination, must have acquired them. Curious to see what had wrought this change in John Jarrett, she opened the unpadlocked gate and approached the farmhouse. The short drive, which used to be a muddy track, was trimly gravelled beneath the frost. The house, cleared of random wooden lean-to sheds, encroaching brambles and the surrounding clutter of farm machinery, stood revealed in seemly plainness and newly pointed stonework, with at least one new sash window (where one of the sheds had been) and with what only Edith's memories of its previous appearance made recognizable to her as a new stone-tiled roof. Edith rang the doorbell and waited for the only explanation she could for the moment think of, an unsuspected Mrs John Jarrett, newly arrived no doubt and wonderfully armed with all that was needed to tame, subdue, civilize and entirely reorganize the Ishmael of Edith's recollection. It was a man who opened the door, a tall man with greying hair and a lean, lightly tanned face, wearing narrow checked tweed trousers and a yellow pullover; he looked inquiringly at her for no more than a few seconds before stretching wide his arms in welcome and saying with evident delight, 'But I know you!'

Alfred was about to get into his car when Edith returned; he was holding two packets of photographs marked DO NOT BEND in large red letters. The back seat of the car seemed full of dogs.

'Sorry,' Edith said. 'I hope you weren't waiting.'

'It's all right, we'll catch the 12 o'clock post, it's just that I've got to get these off.'

'The thing is, John Jarrett's sold the farm, and Charles Warburton's bought it. You remember him, don't you? You wouldn't believe how nice he's making it.'

'Charles Warburton?'

'Perhaps you never knew him. I used to see him ages ago, at parties, he was a sort of friend of Johnny's, but nicer than most of Johnny's friends. I've asked him to come and have a drink some time. He's full of ideas about things to do around here.'

'What sort of things?'

'Oh, nothing much, really. Anyway, you'll like him. And you should see the house. Apparently it was all in an incredible mess.'

'John was never exactly house-proud. Nor much of a farmer, really. More of a horse-dealer. I wonder where he's gone. I'll ask in the pub, he was always in there.'

In fact Alfred did remember Charles Warburton; not well, but well enough to feel apprehensive. The name had disquieting associations. Good old Charlie Warburton. Everyone knew Charlie. In the world, that was, of gentlemen's clubs and amusing people who knew a lot of other amusing people and were not much interested in anyone else, who shared private jokes and went shooting with each other and had responsible well-paid jobs and group holidays with their wives in rented houses in France, and were all, well, jolly nice. Except that they made Alfred feel inadequate, and at the same time aware of being quite different, so that he felt like a child who wanted to make it known that he wouldn't play with those other children even if they asked him, which they were clearly not going to do. He resented being made to feel like that, and consequently disliked that sort of person more than perhaps they deserved. Edith, on the other hand, got on with them perfectly well. She always had, even after her divorce from Johnny and a career which took her into quite different circles. Though really the dreadful Derek (in Alfred's view), her second husband who had so energetically supported, if not master-minded, her political campaign, had been affiliated to Charles Warburton's world, if not exactly a straight up-and-down member of it. Alfred hoped Edith was not going to enter into too enthusiastic a new friendship. He wished she had brought Hubert with her, or Sarah. Edith was such a believer in action. Rightly, he supposed, since she had had a certain amount of success that way, being born responsible, a good citizen, inevitably a magistrate, less inevitably a founder member and for a time the only Parliamentary representative of the Independent Citizens Party, the Party of Common Sense and Co-operation, energetic, efficient, effective; she might have done anything.

Alfred knew very well that Edith thought he ought to have been more ambitious himself, and he felt he was open to reproach on that score, but he could not think what to do about it at this late stage in his life. When he was with Lydia he would have thought ambition meaningless because there was only today and he and Lydia were what the magazines

33

called 'TODAY'S PEOPLE'. He had turned against all that afterwards, but he could not think it much worse than politics; at least, the way they had done it, it had been quite pretty. But how could they ever have thought it had anything you could call substance? Significance – a little perhaps, substance none.

'No indeed, not John Jarrett, that I don't.' Mrs Weeks ironing, steam rising, smell of clean laundry. 'I don't know anything of him, nothing at all, who he sold the house to or what. I wouldn't speak to him, that's why, I never have ever since the way he treated Josie Martin, poor Mrs Martin's girl, that was my friend, Mrs Martin I mean was my friend, Elsie she was, we went into service together, right after the war it was, and her father said to her you do that if you want but you'll regret it, the girls are all going into the factories now, there's none of them going into service, you'll not get a husband that way, they want girls that work in factories and know what's what, that's what he said and not two years went by but he was proved wrong. Ernie Martin was as good a husband as you could have hoped for, good job, steady fellow, better than I got anyway. And Josie was a nice enough girl until she got the horses.'

'Horses?' Edith said in surprise, 'Did she take to gambling, then?'

'Not her. She rode them, that's what. Mad about ponies. Always up there with John Jarrett. He used to buy them in sales, the last lot, you know, going cheap, because he liked them, couldn't resist them. But he never rode them, wasn't interested. He could shoe them, did quite a bit of smithying. They all used to take their horses to him, the hunting people. I've seen Sir George up there and all of them. But the girls couldn't keep away, whether it was John Jarrett or those half-wild ponies, there they were day after day till all hours, hanging about making jumps in the field, galloping round the place, falling off so he could carry them into the house.

Oh yes, don't you look so shocked, young Doris, I know what young girls are, I've been one. Falling off on purpose, that's what they went in for, and grooming the horses, curry-combing and that, mucking out, that's what they called it – mucking about, more like it – and that Josie Martin was one of them, bold as may be, pregnant before she ever left school, that was Josie, and did she care? Not a farthing. Her mother was left with the baby and she upped and off to London saying her life was ruined for love of that John Jarrett, and there he sat as shameless as may be, saying she wouldn't marry him and what was he to do, and the next thing it's Lynne from the other side of the village. You know, Doris, her father used to bake the bread for the shop before they only had the sliced, Lynne was her name, she had a baby. And there was another the next year, that Chrissie Hale, ever such a nice girl, well mannered, had a good job with the shoe people. That was only the half of it. That John Jarrett. They used him, those girls, they just used him, they can get it on the National Health, supplementary benefits and all that they get, they don't mind, no shame at all they haven't.'

'So it's really John Jarrett who was hard done by, not Josie Martin after all?' put in Edith quickly, hoping to stop the flow.

'Weak, like all men, that's what he was, thought himself handsome. I've nothing against him personally. I don't speak to him because Elsie Martin was my friend. Someone's got to keep up some kind of standards.'

'So there's a whole generation of young Jarretts growing up all over the village?'

Mrs Jupp, putting away the Hoover, gave Edith an anxious glance out of her good eye. 'You don't want to believe everything she says,' she said, almost in a whisper. 'She doesn't always mean it.'

'I certainly do mean it. Who do you think the father of Josie Martin's baby was, then? And if you know so much about it, why did he sell his farm? If you know so much about it.'

35

'I think I did hear he got a good price for it, that's all. I never did know about those rumours.'

'He sold it because he had no time to look after it, being always after the girls. That's not rumour. Exaggeration, that's as may be.'

'Exaggeration?' said Edith. 'You, Mrs Weeks? Surely not.'

'I'm always true to the spirit of the thing, that's what your father used to say. Grace, your mother would say, you're elaborating, that's what she'd say, elaborating. And your father would say, Grace is true to the spirit of the thing. And that's the spirit of John Jarrett, I'm telling you.'

Mrs Jupp, having tidied away the cleaning things, fetched her mother's fur-lined boots and the ancient plimsolls she herself favoured for driving, and placed their assorted coats, scarves, gloves, handbags, shopping bags and spare plastic rain-hats on the kitchen table in preparation for departure. Mrs Weeks ironed a tea-towel with a final flourish, switched off the iron and moved over to assume the scarlet woollen coat which Mrs Jupp held out for her. Mrs Jupp then folded the ironing board, stood the iron on a shelf to cool and murmured to Edith, 'I've put the shepherd's pie in the top oven.'

'Do you cook for him now, then? What luxury my brother lives in.'

Mrs Jupp said modestly, 'I did a little for the freezer last week when we knew you were coming.'

'She's always had a feel for cooking,' said Mrs Weeks complacently. 'She gets it from me.'

Pulling on her gloves, she swept out into the bright cold air, followed by the furiously blushing Mrs Jupp.

'What a monster,' said Edith aloud, leaning on the Aga, thinking of laying the table for lunch, thinking also of John Jarrett with his dark, piratical looks and his soft voice and shy evasive eyes. He had a slight speech impediment, was rather slow perhaps, not like his father, a highly competent farmer whom Edith as a child had found alarming. John Jarrett was such a gentle fellow no one could be afraid of him, but it was true that he was handsome. It was he who as a very young man had persuaded his father to allow Lydia to take over the farmyard and fill it all summer long with her friends and their comings and goings. He had been there himself a lot of the time. It had not occurred to her before, but perhaps Lydia too had rolled in the hay with John Jarrett. Edith pushed herself away from the Aga and began briskly to lay the table. The thought of anyone betraying Alfred was extremely disagreeable.

Alfred, having posted his photographs to the publications which had asked him for pictures of the great freeze-up for their city-bound readers, looked in at the pub to be told that John Jarrett was sure to be in later, and, leaving his car by the green, took the dogs up the track behind the pub which led to the high plateau behind the village. The sky had become a bright, cloudless blue and the flat fields spread beneath its immensity were lightly covered with floating swathes of milky mist as the frost began to melt, though the branches of the few small clumps of trees were still outlined in white. Seeing the dogs race ahead of him, leaving their tracks in the melting frost on the grass, Alfred breathed deeply of the painfully cold air, as if it might numb unwelcome thoughts.

Being with Edith in the house in which they had grown up stirred memories of earlier times which he sometimes thought were best forgotten. Suddenly now in the cold he was remembering school; perhaps it was to avoid the thought of his mother, whose death in his absence came to him like a familiar touch on the sciatic nerve most days anyway but of whom he tried not to think consciously too often, because when he did he sometimes felt a storm of pity for her which he knew to be a profitless emotion, since there was nothing he could do for her now. He seldom thought of his school-days; most of the time he had been bored, though his last year or two had been happy enough. Now he was momentarily back at the time when having being educated for his first few years quietly enough at the village school, suddenly he was away from home, sleeping in an unfamiliar place, herded together with a mob of boys whose knowing ways revealed an understanding of an unfamiliar and apparently hostile world which it seemed impossible that he could ever hope to equal. They knew where things were, how things worked, which master was which and how best to pester or placate him, how to wheedle extras out of Matron, how, horrifyingly, to make Alfred cry. So he learned not to cry, or only occasionally in the lavatory after his mother, herself pale and falsely cheerful, had brought him back after a Sunday at home. He learned his way about the place and its still largely inexplicable rituals, and he acquired a friend, David Molesworth, known as Moley and the most popular boy in the class.

Much later it struck Alfred in retrospect that Moley had had certain things in common with Lydia. He was beautiful, for instance, and a little mysterious, and occasionally hysterical. He was something of a leader, not because of any apparent ambition of his own, but because his volatility and charm made people expect it of him, and since he very much wished to be liked he responded by ordering people about; they loved it. 'Moley says . . .', 'I'm doing it for Moley . . .', 'Moley's calling a meeting . . .' Moley called meetings to make plots, and since he in fact had very few ideas about things to do, preferring to froth along on the top of the tide, Alfred as his second in command became the source of enterprise. Alfred had reached this position by laughing at Moley's jokes and feeding him with leads for further witticisms; he had aspired to it because Moley had from the first seemed to him entirely lovable. He gave him an affection and trust which, though it contained an element of physical attraction which was slightly disturbing but about which he preferred not to think, was what a loved and hitherto protected ten-year-old boy thought of as friendship. Moley in a wild mood when laughter became inadequate would howl like a wolf, telling how Matron in giving him a spoonful of Radio Malt had spilt some on her capacious front and what she had said when he offered to lick it off and what had happened when Mr Gregson the maths teacher came in and how Matron had blushed scarlet, tales which were nothing without his mimicry and not much with it but which cheered and charmed his easily infatuated audience. Moley's meetings all one summer term were devoted to the elaboration of a plan, originally Alfred's, for a mass breakout on the evening of the staff party. Security would be light as senior prefects were traditionally invited to the party, and such staff as cared whether the boys kept to their beds or not would be, according to Alfred's optimistic estimate, roaring drunk after a glass or two of the headmaster's medium dry Amontillado sherry. The fine-tuning of the plan went into the selection of groups and the allotting of destinations. Alfred's idea was that if they split up into groups of five and made their way out of the locality in a variety of different directions, by train or bus, on foot or on bicycles, there was more chance of some at least getting through and reaching their homes, so that it would be impossible for the school to cover up the scandal. A boy called Oakley, who even at the age of ten knew that his ambition was to work for Lord Beaverbrook, was appointed press officer and allotted a portion of the pooled pocket money so that he could alert the world's press from a telephone box.

Excitement mounted through the fine summer of 1942, while armies fought and died in the Libyan desert and in front of Stalingrad, and bombs fell in thousands on Coventry and Cologne. Away on the borders of Wales all that, though known about, was unimaginable, even by boys whose parents were part of it. 'Wizard prang,' they would say of their planned escape, most of them unaware of the relationship between their current slang and the language of the RAF pilots whose exploits they admired but took for granted, never supposing a pilot could do anything other than shoot down the enemy and win, easy peasy, just as they would do if they had the chance; but since from their small kindly hills they saw little sign of battle, the chief and for most of them their only interest in the war was the question as to which of their teachers might be German spies. Ceaseless vigilance disclosed that Mr Harben, a solitary and depressive man who was in charge of woodwork, was probably sending signals to the German bombers by flashing lights at night from the woodwork room where he spent late lonely evenings finishing off the egg holders and bird tables which the boys would later take home as their own unaided work. The headmaster, a man for all his faults not unsympathetic to small boys, thanked them for reporting the matter and reassured them solemnly that he had personally vetted all the staff as to their loyalty and patriotism but would have a word with Mr Harben about the chink in the blackout curtains.

Alfred meanwhile was happily involved with timetables and maps. He had discovered that there would be a new moon on the night in question; it seemed a good augury. Moley enlarged on the prospect of national search parties, the public humiliation of the headmaster, the outrage of the school governors, the eventual closing of the school, until his followers were screwed up to a fine pitch of resolve. And then Moley went home one Sunday and did not come back. He was ill, Matron said, a chill on the liver she'd been told; he would be back soon. He did not come back. Matron said it was mild hepatitis. No one thought for a moment that they could make the great escape without their leader. The term came uneventfully to an end.

Moley was back the next term, as sparkling as ever, but the escape never happened. The project was put on ice; there was an idea that it might be resuscitated the following summer. In the meantime the long autumn term dragged on; the evenings darkened. One afternoon Alfred and Moley were idly bouncing a tennis ball between them in an empty classroom. Moley threw it at the wall, Alfred failed to catch it as it bounced back. It landed on one of the little china inkwells which were a part of each desk in those days before the invention of the biro. When Alfred picked it up from the floor, one side of it was wet with ink.

'Yuk. Wipe it off,' said Moley.

Alfred did, on the bare wall behind him, leaving a surprisingly large blue circle. Shocked by the size of the blemish, they nevertheless agreed that it was a filthy wall anyway (dirty cream paint, scratched and marked, though not until then by ink) and went on playing. In came the rest of the class, in came the maths master, Mr Gregson. 'Who made that filthy mark?' Silence. 'Whoever did it must come and see me in the staff room after lessons.' They did not go, of course. How could they, not having held up their hands at the first opportunity, 'Please, sir, me, sir'?

The weeks which followed seemed now to be bathed in a sickly retrospective light but had seemed much as usual at the time. The scandal grew; there was nothing much going on that term. Encouraged by the authorities, the campaign to find the culprit was pursued with mounting fervour. At its head were Moley and Alfred, where they were expected to be. Swept along by events they hardly discussed the thing among themselves. 'It'll fade out soon,' they had muttered on the first day, without really looking at each other. But they themselves, because it was expected of them, were part of the movement to prevent it fading out. Between the high yew hedges in the garden beside the tennis courts someone had set up a seat of justice, messengers were sent out to call in suspects, the guiltless were cross-examined with fearsome solemnity. Moley and Alfred, though associated with this campaign, were a little apart from it, Oakley and one or two of the others who had been active in the escape plans being the chief instigators. Naturally neither Moley nor Alfred came under suspicion, Moley because he was the most popular boy in the class, Alfred because he was Moley's friend.

Still young enough to find the dividing line between what

was so and what ought to have been so easily blurred, Alfred soon more or less believed that the mark on the wall had nothing to do with him and lost himself in his usual schoolboy activities, each night too tired to do other than fall straight to sleep. Until the morning when Moley came into his dormitory early, whispered, 'I've told them,' and ran out of the room. Dressing quickly, his fertile mind busy with exonerating details, Alfred hurried down to where the morning run, performed in pairs on the tarmac drive round a central oval of grass, took place every day before breakfast; Alfred and Moley habitually ran together. Moley was standing with a group of two or three other boys. They did not look at Alfred as he approached. He began, 'We can say . . .' Moley said, 'I'm running with Green.' A senior boy came up and said to Alfred, 'The headmaster wants to see you before prayers.'

'I'm running with Green.' Only then had Alfred begun to realize the extent of his own delusion. Moley had not made the mark on the wall; Alfred had. They had not been, as so often before, in a scrape together. Alfred had been the offender, Moley only the witness.

The headmaster was a sentimental man, who had observed with pleasure the friendship between two lively little boys, and indeed the particular devotion of the quieter one to the more ebullient. He looked out of the window and said, 'I am afraid this is rather sad for you.' Rooks rose from windtossed elms beyond the playing field. 'I am afraid you have lost a friend.' Dawn on the desolate illimitable plain. 'Perhaps it's punishment enough. We all make mistakes sometimes, don't we? Run along now.' Turn, walk to the door, open it, shut it behind you.

Had the headmaster said something similar in prayers? Alfred could not remember. Certainly the news became known – no beating, no punishment at all. The headmaster must have been mad. Alfred was sent to Coventry. Green, passing him in the passage, hissed, 'You swore on the Bible.'

Perhaps he had. Doggedly he began the long sentence of solitude.

Moley did not come back to school the following term. Alfred's sentence was not lifted until the term which succeeded it, when Green told him that he had talked the matter over with his elder brother during the holidays and decided it was wrong to continue the ban on communication. 'I think you are a proud person and must have suffered,' said Green (they were both eleven by now). 'And besides we have all got to work hard for our Common Entrance.'

'Thank you, Green. That's decent of you.'

Moley wrote him a letter describing his new school, which he said had super food. 'P.S. I hope you have forgiven me.' Alfred wrote back at length with all the news, adding, 'P.S. Of course I have forgiven you – what for, anyway??!' He did not hear from Moley again.

By the time he left to go to his public school, Alfred had grown to six foot, a quiet and cautious boy, not too bad at lessons. Certain things had been stamped indelibly on his heart, the curve of a dark eyebrow as it sprang away from the delicate bridge of a nose, the light dust of fine hairs on a cheekbone, a joyful, easy smile.

'I've asked Charles Warburton to come and have a drink tomorrow,' said Edith, as Alfred walked into the kitchen. 'Before lunch, I thought, rather than this evening, because of the weather.'

'Good.'

'You'll like him, I know.'

'Yes.' Alfred picked up the newspapers. 'Is this one of Hubert's days?'

'I don't know. I haven't looked.'

'He's awfully good still, Hubert. He's the only political correspondent I ever read.'

'He's been at it a long time, he's got very good sources. I suppose it's difficult not to get stale, but he seems to be quite good at recycling the same article. It's an awful life really, all gossip, especially at the moment.'

'He loves it, though, doesn't he?'

'You do love politics when you're in it. You have the illusion that it matters.'

'Listen, I've remembered something awful. The vicar usually comes on Wednesday evenings, to play chess. Shall I put him off?'

'Not Raven? He can't still be alive?'

'Yes, yes, going strong.'

'Isn't there a retiring age for vicars?'

'I think he probably has retired. It doesn't seem to have made any difference. Perhaps he doesn't get paid.'

'Does anyone go to church?'

'The parish has been merged with five others, so no one really knows where the services are. So old Raven just goes on. There is another vicar really, a proper one, but he hardly ever comes here. I dare say he's happy enough to leave it to Raven.'

'D'you ever go?'

'Now and then, to show willing. He gets through the service in no time. Not that I think he's lost faith in God, exactly, more in people. But he's a vicious chess player.'

'Don't put him off. I've got some work to do.'

'Are you sure? I mean he really is tremendously old.'

'Never mind. I'll cook something wonderful. Has he got any teeth?'

'Splendid teeth. I'll give him a ring to remind him to put them in.'

Edith thought that Alfred should do more with his life than play chess once a week with an old man who had to be reminded to put his teeth in. After lunch he wandered off upstairs saying he had a few things to finish, and Edith went into the sitting-room, which was tidy and smelt pleasantly of furniture polish after the attentions of Mrs Weeks and Mrs Jupp, and sat down to read the newspaper and allow her

irritation full rein. Ever since he had been born, Edith had
believed that Alfred was a person of exceptional value and
originality, and in her scheme of things such a person should
first of all do something about it and then either be generally
acclaimed or make some money, preferably both. Her irritation arose from her unwillingness to see that such thinking
led to the conclusion that Alfred's life was a wasted life. She
refused to accept this, but had to recognize that time might
be running short. She knew that Alfred was appreciated by
some people as a good photographer, but what was photography? Anyone could point a camera; you could hardly call
it a career. She had always thought those fashionable photographers of the sixties were frauds, cashing in on the
throw-away culture of the times. And then the full life was
meant to include marriage, and children. Alfred would have
been a good father; look how kind he had always been to
Sarah and then to Sarah's children. And all he had done was
wander about the world and then take the line of least
resistance by more or less squatting in their parents' house. He
had done nothing to it except for the barest maintenance;
apart from a few improvements which she herself had made, it
was much as it had been in their parents' day, only a good deal
untidier. And after all he was still good-looking, distinguished,
not at all fat (unlike Hubert). Supposing she brought the
school down here, or rather some selected groups, and supposing Rose Brown came to help. Now Rose was a thoroughly
nice woman, intelligent, handsome, vivacious. She spoke
perfect French, had written a biography of Madame de
Sévigné, rather a dull biography as a matter of fact, but
there would be no need for Alfred to read it, and she was a
widow, not a divorcee, which was good because there would
be less likelihood of a residue of bitterness against the male
sex. Rose would soon reorganize Alfred, and then the two of
them could run the country branch of the language school;
they might expand it, have conferences, and then eventually
Sarah could take it over, which would mean she could leave

45

that ghastly public relations world and the children could benefit from the country air. There was no doubt about it, Edith thought, she would have to raise the subject of the farmyard again with Charles Warburton, but perhaps without at this stage mentioning it to Alfred; there was no point in involving him until matters were further advanced. Charles Warburton seemed to have some ideas of his own, but no doubt the schemes could be reconciled; he seemed easy enough to talk to.

5

Lawrence Raven was a short man, but solid. There was something about the set of his head on his shoulders which was authoritative, as if he had once been given a prize for best of breed in a class of little black Welsh cattle. He was white-haired now, with a well-groomed fringe of white beard round his lower jaw and chin. This gave him an air not so much old-fashioned as medieval; with his broad cheekbones, wide mouth and overhanging brows he could have been a lively misericord on an upturned choir seat in a Gothic cathedral. He kept himself very clean, because he was aware of not having a woman to look after him, and did not want his standards to deteriorate in his old age. In preparation for his evening with Alfred and Edith he shaved for the second time that day, and scrubbed his face until his cheeks were pink and shining. Then he washed the top of his head, which was bald; he could not see it, or at least not without much awkward manipulation of mirrors, and he was afraid of forgetting it, and disclosing to the gaze of those many who were taller than himself patches of unclean or scrofulous skin framed by the snowy white hair which grew round the sides and back of his head.

Shaving was an exercise of skill which he enjoyed, though it was his habit to go into Wells once a month for a professional shave and haircut. The beard really began above his ears, passed in front of them, and descended in a clearly delineated fringe round the side of his face, deepening to a couple of inches under his chin. Round his mouth, he was entirely clean-shaven. The effect of his strong, almost pugnacious, face was diminished when he smiled, because he had trouble with his teeth. The archdeacon of the diocese many years ago, a vain man who had long since been translated to higher office, had once told him that a man was well-advised to have all his teeth out in middle age because dentures maintained the contours of a youthful face, rather than allowing the cheeks to fall inwards as the teeth rotted. Lawrence had thought this advice too drastic and had not immediately followed it, but he had borne it in mind to the extent that whenever he had had any trouble with a tooth he had insisted that it should be pulled out and no nonsense, with the result that he had had no teeth at all for some years. Unfortunately he found his false ones from the first so uncomfortable that when he was alone he took them out, and since he was alone a good deal of the time he had never become used to them. Thus without his teeth he looked very old indeed, and with them his smile had a ghastly insincerity, which arose from his in fact unfounded fear that they would fall out. When he went to supper with Alfred, on their regular chess evenings, or when he himself provided the supper in his bungalow, he usually started the evening with his teeth in but often removed them during the course of the game, believing quite erroneously that Alfred did not notice. The bungalow had been built in the garden of the Rectory, a big Victorian house which had been sold to a middle-management man from a biscuit firm in Bristol, whose wife was a teacher with a rasping voice, the sound of which over the wattle fence Lawrence particularly disliked.

In fact he did not much like women at all. Such sexual experience as he had had, whether with his own or with the other sex, was now so remote in time that if there had been (which he doubted) any aspect of it which was other than laughable or disgusting he had long forgotten it; but it was not in their physical manifestation that women failed to please him so much as in their opinions. Even when he agreed with them (which did occasionally happen), it was the vehemence of their views which appalled him. He was a sociable man and often went to see his acquaintances in the neighbourhood, many of them clergymen living in retirement in Wells, and besides that he had two old college friends with whom he frequently communicated on the telephone about some very advanced crossword puzzles, and he belonged to a sketching club (of which a majority of the members was in fact female) which went abroad as a group once a year to sketch, usually in France; but wherever he went his experience was that where there was vehemence there was a woman, where there was mildness there was a man. He preferred mildness. He had known Edith as a child but had seen very little of her since; he approached the evening with some apprehension. He knew that she had been a Member of Parliament at one time, and he thought she probably continued to play some part in public life, though he could not quite think what that part might be. He hoped very much that she would not become vehement about women priests. Not that he was against women priests, of course not; he just preferred not to talk about them. Or think about them really.

He was wheeling his bicycle out of the garage, having locked the back door, when he heard the telephone ring. He unlocked the door and went back into the house to find that it was Alfred, to say that the roads were too slippery for bicycling in the dark and that he would come and fetch him in the car. A nice man, Alfred, a nice mild man. Lawrence settled his round tweed hat firmly on his head (it was rather too small for him) and waited obediently to be fetched.

Edith had made a cheese soufflé. She was a good though infrequent cook. In London she often ate out so that her meals at home tended to be self-denying snacks which she hoped would prevent her getting fat; when Hubert came round it was usually he who did the cooking. It was some time since she had used an Aga and she was pleased that the soufflé was perfect. Making the best of the prospect of an unexciting evening, she had thrown herself into the domestic mode, turned up the heating in the dining-room, laid the

49

table with extra care, and transported from the kitchen window sill the most orderly of Alfred's pelargoniums. Most of them had spread recklessly under his liberal regime, but she found a pink one of more formal habit, and dug out for it from the back of the kitchen cupboard a Wedgwood cache pot she had not seen for years.

Lawrence Raven, who usually ate in the kitchen with Alfred on their chess evenings, smiled rather desperately and rubbed his hands together, saying, 'Well, well,' several times. Alfred, amused to see Edith behaving so correctly, watched her draw Lawrence out with gentle inquiries about himself. This she did to such good effect that details of Lawrence's life emerged which were quite unfamiliar to Alfred – how many funerals he conducted a year (few), how many baptisms (few), how he came to be a priest, having been an art student in the nineteen-twenties, studying under Tonks at the Slade; he used to listen to Donald Soper preaching at Tower Hill in his lunch hour, and when it became clear to him that he would never earn a living as a painter, he thought he would become a Methodist minister. His mother had said it would kill his grandfather, who had been an archdeacon in the Church of England, and so he was ordained into that church instead, and was later an army chaplain. After that he had worked in the East End with Toc H, and found out what an admirable and of course at the same time in some ways difficult man Tubby Clayton was who had started the Toc H movement to carry on the work begun in the war at Talbot House, close to the Ypres salient, where fighting men could come in their brief rests from the front. And he was a Welshman, Lawrence Raven. That Alfred did know, because it was he who had told Alfred and Lydia how beautiful Pembrokeshire was, where the Raven grandparents had lived, and that was why they had gone there, and then poor Lawrence had felt guilty, but what had happened there could have happened anywhere. And Edith was saying, 'That's why you have such a good voice. For speaking, I mean.'

50

'For singing too, your father used to tell me. But it is useful to have a little of the Welsh intonation, because it takes away the class connotation. One has the more open vowel. So many of my friends have told me they can't concentrate in church because the parson's voice is either too lah-di-dah or puts them in mind of the West Midlands police. Also, you know, Welsh people have very clear diction, useful for reading those virtually incomprehensible bits of the Old Testament.' Lawrence, feeling increasingly relaxed, drained his glass of Alfred's good wine, secure in the knowledge that it would soon be refilled. 'It was helpful in the East End too, a bit of Welsh. I think I probably had more of it then, and being Welsh put you on the sidelines. The Jews thought you understood their problems because you would have been told at some time in your life that Taffy was a Welshman, Taffy was a thief. There were still Jews in the East End in those days who spoke only Yiddish.'

'Oh, if it was only Jews now,' said Edith, changing the plates.

'When I go to get my hair cut in Wells,' said Lawrence, 'there's such a good-looking boy who washes one's hair. He's of Kenyan origin apparently, but he must come from one of those very handsome warrior tribes. And then when he speaks it's the purest rustic Somerset. Quite charming.'

'It's all a little more complicated in London,' said Edith.

'I'm afraid so,' said Lawrence so humbly that Edith, having urged him to help himself to steak and kidney pie, felt it necessary to say, 'I made a complete idiot of myself over race in London. In fact I really what you might say buggered up my whole career.'

'Oh, but you had a career,' said Lawrence earnestly. 'Think of that. I'd have buggered up any career if I'd had one but I never did.'

'You bury the dead and christen the children,' said Alfred, pleased by Lawrence's robust reaction to Edith's language. 'Isn't that a career?'

'Very few dead. And only the children of the heathen. The proper incumbent here makes an awful fuss about christening the children of parents who aren't regular church-goers. Cutting off your nose to spite your face, I call that. In fact he's legally obliged to do it whether he likes it or not, but not many people know that and even if they do he makes such heavy weather of it that when they hear there's an old fool who doesn't visit the sins of the fathers on the children they take the easy way out. He loathes me. There's nothing to compare with the hatred of one member of an institution for another.'

'My goodness, yes,' said Edith, who was enjoying herself more than she had expected to. 'It's only the party members who prevent politicians on the same side from assassinating each other. In the ICP we didn't have enough ordinary members to keep us in order. No structure. Derek was always going on in his military way about the chain of command. He was right really, but he couldn't do anything about it. We collapsed in an awful quarrelsome muddle after I lost my seat in the general election, and he wasn't there to help.'

'But you set the pattern for the Social Democratic party,' said Lawrence. 'Lib Dems or whatever they are now.'

'Well they absorbed us, such as we were, but none of us really ever got a footing there. And then they all started quarrelling too.'

'Why was it race, Edith, that defeated you?' said Alfred. 'I was living in Italy then, wasn't I? Anyway, I know I was out of the country. I thought it was just the usual thing, people voting for minority parties at by-elections and then reverting to the others at general elections.'

'It may have been partly that. But I got into a ghastly scrape over race. Play groups were my downfall really, multiracial play groups, mothers and babies clubs – it worked so well in Kensington where I started, and then suddenly this funny little group in North London said why didn't I stand for Parliament there, so off I went and quite unexpectedly won it and I suppose it went to my head. Anyway, the things that worked in Kensington were considered patronizing and neo-colonialist, and I didn't take the trouble to find out what had been going on before and why there was so much infighting, I just went barging on. The National Front moved in in a big way when they knew race was on the agenda. It was just about the time when they first appeared and no one could quite think what to do about them. I just got crushed between the warring factions. The Labour man played his cards quite well and won the seat back. I should have found out what a minefield it all was before I got involved.'

'Well, you've got the language school,' said Alfred. 'Isn't that race relations?'

'Not in the sense people now use that phrase. But it is in a way, I suppose. Quite a few of them seem to keep in touch with each other afterwards.'

'So you can rejoice,' said Lawrence. 'Do you remember how your father would say that? "Rejoice, rejoice!" Rushing into choir practice late in the icy-cold church. "Rejoice!" Do you remember?'

'It was infuriating,' said Edith. 'Struggling with some awful holiday essay and he bursting in telling one to rejoice in the Lord.'

'I think he was telling himself,' said Alfred. 'Even in those days he can't have been as joyful as that all the time. His best songs are the sad ones.'

Edith gathered up the plates, took them out into the kitchen and began to make coffee. Alfred followed her with some dishes and she murmured, 'Is he all right?'

'His cup is full. His bowl as well. I may never get him home.'

'I'll make up a bed in the spare room when I go up.'

'Don't bother. I'll just roll him up in a rug.'

But much later as she lay in bed Edith heard them pass her door, rather noisily, and go into the spare room where she had indeed put sheets on the bed and turned on the electric fire (which judging by the strong smell of burning dust which it emitted had not been used for some time).

'Splendid, splendid. What a wonderful person Edith has become, so good of you both . . .' Lawrence's voice, no less sincere for being slightly slurred, reached her through the wall.

I wonder if I ought to take a pill, she thought, I am dreaming much too strongly. It is the feeling of coming home when it is not home; everything seems to mean something else. But she could not remember whether she had brought any sleeping pills with her and was anyway slipping back into whatever it was she had been dreaming about when the voices woke her – something about a battle, and a round-faced clergyman who was not Lawrence Raven, and her father lying on a bed, groaning.

Alfred sat up in bed reading a biography of Robert Maxwell. His brain, though slightly blurred by port, was still too active for sleep, and he had no wish to lie awake regretting his moves in the three games of chess in each of which he had been soundly beaten. There was also at the back of his mind some kind of uncomfortable feeling left by Edith's casual revelations about her political activities. He had been remote from English life at the time, relishing his isolation on a Tuscan hillside, trying to make his vines and olives pay their way and at intervals wandering the Apennines like Harold in Italy.

And there had been Edith down in the arena, joining battle, though lightly armed. She had written to him:

You'll never believe it, I'm standing for Parliament. Don't worry, I won't get in. It turned out there were these people who'd got themselves together and put up an Independent candidate at the last election and he (the candidate) had had enough and didn't want to stand again, and I've made such an exhibition of myself lately on the Council banging on about schools and housing and stuff and getting a lot of publicity because of the success of the street play group schemes that they'd heard of me, these dear people, and thought I'd be just the kind of idiot to take it on. Which I am, of course. They're a funny lot, mostly early symptoms of the gentrification which is getting under way in that part of North London, people with consciences and theories and a good deal of naïve optimism and not much idea of how to organize anything. Some of them are potentially quite tiresome and some I really like (being that way myself, I suppose, except I honestly believe my little bit of experience has made me quite efficient, and I do have some idea of how to work towards a goal – I mean how to compromise and not be petty, and how to think about what's a priority and what's not). Also I have to admit I do simply love making speeches. When I first stood for the Council, I went on a course of public speaking. Did I ever tell you about it? It was so funny. There was an ex-actor who'd gone into advertising and started these courses when he retired. We did breathing exercises and practised shouting and were told how to stand and how to deal with hecklers and how to never answer questions, just say what you were going to say anyway and pretend it's an answer. Then it's how to do your hair and how to smile and what to do with your hands – body language, it's called – much more important than the other sort apparently. So if you do have something you want to say, you say it again and again and again and again. It's a performance, like singing, and I'm just never nervous, the problem is to stop me.

But that part of London is pretty awful, you know. I don't quite know how it got like that (but I mean to find out). There are some lovely squares and what were once highly respectable houses, all made into horrible bedsitting-rooms with vicious landlords and surrounded by a sprawl of early-twentieth-century development and abandoned by decent folk and so shabby and dilapidated and now full of immigrants – not spicy and vibrant etc. like ethnic quarters in other great capitals, but down-at-heel, forgotten places and dripping basements and traffic and people who don't dare to apply for the state benefits they're entitled to in case they get deported (except for the ones who are busy cheating the system and probably ought to be deported). NOT GOOD. So I intend to make as much fuss about everything as possible until my dear dotty supporters sack me for getting even less votes than their last candidate.

And then of course she had astonished everyone and got herself elected. She wrote to Alfred that it was a fluke because the left-wing vote was split, but nevertheless there she was, in Parliament, and he had always assumed that her subsequent career had been highly creditable, leading to her being taken seriously and put on boards and committees and all that sort of thing for ever afterwards. She had said she did not expect to keep her seat for more than one Parliament, since her winning it had been the result of a particular situation within a particular constituency, but she might have expected to find another seat, particularly after the founding of the SDP, only by that time there had been the trouble with Derek. All the same, she had surely no reason to think herself as a failure. Alfred did not like that. He wanted to tell her that it was a mistake to think of oneself in terms of worldly achievements anyway, but he knew he never would. And there was Maxwell going from one scheme to another more and more successfully – until the crash of course, when it had emerged that everyone who had ever had anything to do with him had always known he was really a crook. And yet they had let themselves be convinced by him; it must have been his self-confidence. 'People take you at your own valuation,' Alfred's mother used to say to him, urging him to be more self-assertive, she who was as aggressive in pursuit of her own ends as a grasshopper. *'La Cigale et la fourmi'*. They had learnt La Fontaine's *Fables* as small children with Mademoiselle, who taught at the girls' school where their father taught music and who had given them lessons privately because at the village school they did not teach French. Mademoiselle cried a lot because her family were in German-occupied France and she did not know what had happened to them. Edith was sometimes quite rude to her; but then of course Edith had always been brave. Mademoiselle used to rap their knuckles with a ruler when they made mistakes. *'Savez-vous planter les choux/À la mode de chez nous?'*

Edith had fallen asleep again after hearing the other two coming upstairs, but then she had woken and looked at her watch and found that it was only half past one. She had been to the lavatory, wondering vaguely whether the fact that nowadays she usually had to go at least once in the night when until recently she never used to go at all was something to do with the fact of her increasing age, and whether she ought to worry about it, and whether old age was going to be as horrible as she thought it was. At least she had Sarah, who was both competent and kind – fairly kind, anyway – and would know what to do if she became senile. But who would look after Alfred? It really would be so convenient if Rose Brown would take him in hand; it was simply not desirable that he should go on living alone, having the vicar to supper once a week and then putting him to bed. 'I'll just roll him in a rug,' he had said, quite as if that was what he always had to do. At least he should see a few more people, people like Charles Warburton for instance, who would cheer him up.

It was because she was tired, and was finding herself oddly disorientated by this visit – perhaps because the unexpectedly icy grip of the weather seemed to have fixed everything in some kind of immobility, as if she and Alfred were two specimens in a jar – that she had spoken carelessly about her experiences in the Parliamentary election in which she had lost her seat. She had not meant to give the impression that she had been hounded out amid general contumely; in fact she had only lost to the Labour candidate by a few hundred votes, and had been praised for her campaign by political commentators (by Hubert indeed, although she hardly knew him then). Her characterizing all that time as having ended in tears was really because it had coincided with the trouble with Derek. She wished she had explained at supper that in fact she had had plenty of good experiences in the constituency and that for most of her time in the House of Commons she had been quite childishly excited to find herself there and immeasurably pleased to find how quickly she began, at least in her own estimation, to function usefully. As to her error, it had only been to misjudge someone she had thought a friend. In fact he had been a friend in a way, handsome Lal the Sri Lankan, but he had had his own fish to fry; and, anyway, it was all a long time ago. A lot of things were a long time ago. She went to sleep smiling at the thought of Lawrence Raven saying he had not voted Conservative since Suez; that really was going back a bit. But then she dreamt she was at some kind of demonstration in Trafalgar Square, with friends, cheerful, people coming and going, old and young, a tall old man with a firm, distinguished face saying, 'You're absolutely right, well done,' and a sudden disturbance at one side of the square, and people running and policemen and then booing and shouting and between the shoulders of the policemen who had linked arms the ugly snarling faces shouting, 'Nigger-lover out out out.' Her mother's face, white and shocked, appeared for a moment in the crowd. 'I am transferring my allegiance to Labour,' she was saying. But that was what Lal had said.

★

Lawrence was dreaming of smooth black flesh and a soft Somerset voice saying, 'You going on holiday then this year?' and as the boy leant over it seemed he had no clothes on and Lawrence's gaze was on a level with something not immediately recognizable, something that might have been an exotic plant, a great black orchid, stirring slightly, growing, as in one of those speeded-up natural history films on television, one part of it swelling, extending, to attract humming birds, becoming larger, harder, no. No. Lawrence swam frantically upwards, towards the top of his consciousness, surfaced, and woke up. He turned on the light and saw that either Edith or Alfred had left a bottle of mineral water and a glass by his bed. Could anything be kinder? He poured himself out a glass with an unsteady hand. Everyone had all those instincts, he told himself; naturally, they were only natural. One had to submit them to common sense, and conscience. Even old men in their eighties, men of the cloth at that, had them. And rather than feel anxious at finding himself dreaming about male genitalia he should remind himself that if he were to dream about female private parts he might well fail to recognize them. Perhaps this happened sometimes. He sipped his mineral water. The idea that his unconscious, night after night, might be sending him subversive messages which his conscious mind consistently failed to interpret seemed to him pleasing. He finished his glass of water, turned out the light, and slept soundly until morning.

6

'Well, now he's asked us to dinner,' said Alfred next morning.

'Lawrence Raven?'

'Your ex-husband.'

'Johnny? How frightful. We can't go.'

'I said I'd let them know. He rang up this morning. Friday, he said. Not New Year's Eve because you hate New Year's Eve.'

'Did he say that? How nice of him. To remember, I mean.'

'We'd better go. It'll be me that suffers, I'll have to sit next to Hermione.'

'Poor old Johnny. I suppose I could bear it, if you want to. What's happened to Lawrence?'

'He hitched a lift with the postman. He's always rather embarrassed about staying the night. I'll say yes then, to Johnny.'

Alfred had always liked Johnny. He had been sixteen when Edith had told him that she was engaged, and his astonishment had been at the thought of his eighteen-year-old sister undertaking something so adult as marriage rather than at her choice of husband. He had accepted what seemed to be the general opinion among their neighbours, that this was some kind of triumph for Edith; it was social advancement, in return for which she was expected to bring cheerfulness and in due course heirs to a solid family with a fine estate and a good house. Such was Edith's lack of sophistication at the time that she was surprised by this reaction, and at first annoyed. Her mother, aware of her feelings, struggled to conceal her own satisfaction; it was a measure of her success that a certain private pleasure on this account did creep into

Edith's enjoyment of the wedding preparations. She was prepared to put up with being the envy of her neighbours as long as no one actually mentioned it in her hearing. As to the good house, that was a distant prospect, both Johnny's parents being alive and in good health and neither being disposed to hand over anything prematurely.

When in due course Alfred provoked paternal displeasure by saying after his two years' undistinguished national service in the RAF that he did not want to go to university, it was Johnny who found him a job in the office of a fellow insurance broker in the City, and who reassured Alfred's parents as to the desirability of starting early on the career ladder. So he found himself a bedsitting-room in a lodging house off Victoria Street where he was provided with a large breakfast every morning before he set out to take the tube from St James's Park station to Monument, which was a few minutes' walk from his office in Leadenhall Street. He wore a dark suit, which he had had made for him at a tailor patronized by his father in Wells (it was only later that Johnny introduced him to his much more expensive London tailor) and an uncomfortable stiff white collar and a bowler hat. He soon abandoned the stiff collar in favour of a starched white shirt, but when he lost his bowler hat at a rather disorderly party he once went to straight from his office he replaced it by a better one with a fashionably curled brim. At first he used to carry an umbrella, but he lost so many that he could no longer afford to replace them. His work was undemanding. He was responsible to Humphrey, a friendly family man with years of experience in the insurance market who would send him off every morning with a list of applications from clients for underwriting for a variety of insurance risks. With this Alfred would make a leisurely circuit of the large crowded space which was the Room at Lloyd's, sometimes queueing patiently by some underwriter's box for an opportunity to sit beside him for a few minutes while he decided what percentage of a particular risk he was prepared to take on, and sometimes finding that he could get through the list quite comfortably by halfway through the morning. Since no one expected him to report back to the office before the afternoon this meant that he could repair earlier than usual to the bar at Pimm's in Threadneedle Street, where the atmosphere was convivial. Later on, when he acquired an old MG of doubtful roadworthiness, he would sometimes drive to work, and at lunchtime he would park the car by a particularly convenient bend in the pavement just outside Pimm's. Humphrey, who also lunched at Pimm's on the days when he did not go to the City Universities Club, once made some kind of jocular comment as to the length of time the MG seemed to spend parked outside, and after that Alfred did not leave it there so often.

At the bar of Pimm's, or upstairs in the restaurant (to which Alfred did not always go, contenting himself with a hot sausage at the bar), he would often meet Johnny, and various of Johnny's cheerful friends, and afterwards he would sometimes go with them to drink coffee and play chess at Bunty's; then back to the office for a couple of hours and off to the tube at five. When he noticed that Johnny seemed to be regarded by his friends, many of whom had been at school with him, as what they might have called pretty much of a complete ass, he was unconcerned. Johnny was clearly well liked in spite of this flaw (if flaw it was), and since Edith had always known exactly what she wanted, it was to be presumed that she wanted to be married to a complete ass.

At breakfast in his lodging house, which was rather portentously known as Regency Chambers, Alfred sometimes talked to a man called Austen Underwood, who worked in advertising. He had been sent down from Oxford for riotous behaviour but seemed at first sight very quiet. It soon transpired that the quietness was connected with the riotous behaviour, in that he kept late hours and often had a bad hangover at breakfast time. One evening he asked Alfred to join him for a drink at a nearby pub where he was meeting some friends.

The friends turned out to be undergraduates, who talked Oxford gossip in fast, emphatic voices, affected attitudes of serious irresponsibility and set great store by anything they thought a good remark, being generous in their appreciation of each other's witticisms. It was clear that in their eyes Austen Underwood, whom they called Augustine, was a figure quite at variance with the pallid breakfaster of Regency Chambers; they seemed to look on him as a figure of excess, a desperado of the gambling tables, a relentless pursuer of wild women and exotic night life. Tales of his exploits in these areas would be enlarged upon by his friends in his presence and though he only smiled enigmatically he never denied them, any more than he ever refused a bet. His nights seemed mostly to be devoted to gambling, at that time an illegal activity. There was apparently a mysterious figure who organized games of roulette and *chemin de fer* on a more or less professional basis though in a number of different private houses; these occasions had some kind of sophisticated and slightly dangerous allure for Augustine and he never missed an opportunity to take part. His wins and losses, the latter only slightly exceeding the former, seemed to Alfred exotically large. He remained quiet and pale, wryly humorous, mysteriously knowing. Alfred decided, as he came to know him better, that much of what his friends said of Augustine was pure invention, a private joke which had arisen out of the need to find an explanation for his odd air of authority, which came in fact, in Alfred's view, from his single-mindedness. He was interested in only one thing, which was money, in all its aspects. This overriding interest gave him the slight reserve of the truly dedicated. It made him more impressive than his other attributes could account for; it must have had an effect on his employers too, since they soon raised his salary, and the desperation with which he used to open or fail to open his mail in the mornings abated as his debts were gradually reduced. It was not long before he suggested to Alfred that they should leave Regency Chambers and rent a flat together. Alfred, swayed by the financial light-heartedness of his new friends, agreed. They moved into the top floor of a house in Walpole Street, not far down the King's Road from Sloane Square.

The house belonged to an artists' model called Hope Handyside. She claimed to have sat for Whistler, and when fuddled by alcohol, as she was most evenings, for Alfred Munnings, whose widow was a frequent visitor. If challenged to prove the second of these assertions, since no one could remember any portraits by Munnings which were not of horses, she would imply secret knowledge which would one day astonish the art world, but if a treasure trove of Munnings studies in the nude ever existed it never subsequently came to light. A cheerful old painter called Brown, rather unsteady on his legs, would call in now and then to tell her about a big new commission he was about to get from a Cornish landowner who liked vast panoramas of historical subjects to hang in his ancient halls. Some of these projects had in the past materialized and Hope had been enthroned as Boadicea or some other warrior queen, but the landowner's wife did not share his enthusiasm and the next commission was slow in coming. Brown seemed to have no other patrons, but was never down-hearted; evenings when Hope would shout up the stairs to ask Alfred and Augustine to come down and have a drink because Brown was there were always cheerful occasions. The two old people would gossip about the Chelsea of their youth. 'No social butterflies like you two then,' Hope would say indulgently, coughing and reaching for the gin. 'We were all for art in those days.'

Augustine was not for art at all; he wanted to marry an heiress. But Alfred would sometimes sit on the window seat in Hope's high-ceilinged sitting-room and look in at its apparent muddle of dark furniture, untidy sofas strewn with embroidered or faded velvet cushions, tables covered with dusty ornaments (a coronation mug, a souvenir from Cleethorpes), many small pictures hung at random on the dark green walls, and suddenly a blue silk Chinese shawl with a pattern of silver dragons on it draped round Hope's large, stooping shoulders would seem of a wonderful richness, as if its dimly refulgent colour had come from the palette of a master, and Hope's face, responding to something said from his dark winged chair by the substantial shadow which was Brown, would briefly reveal through the overblown flesh the fine bone structure which had been her pride. He felt grateful to Hope for these moments, which seemed to him obscurely valuable, and because he knew she had not much money he was careful never to be late with his rent. Augustine was quite often late, but then he amused her, so could be said to sing for his supper.

When he had time, Alfred would walk the short distance down the King's Road to Markham Street to see Edith and Johnny, who now had a child, Sarah. Sarah was an excellent baby and Edith an excellent mother; Johnny seemed content to be excluded from their mutual admiration. Edith and Johnny's friends were conventional; when they asked them for drinks, Edith would sometimes introduce Alfred (though with a certain pride) as 'my disreputable brother'. Certainly Alfred's friends were generally more raffish, though Augustine's pursuit of heiresses sometimes took both of them to débutante dances for which Alfred had to hire a dinner jacket or even a tailcoat from Moss Bros in Covent Garden. Eventually his mother found a dinner jacket which had become too tight for his father and had it adapted to fit Alfred. This was Alfred's last visit to the tailor in Wells. He had a suit made by Johnny's London tailor, in a light pepper and salt worsted, with narrow trousers, cuffs on the five-buttoned sleeves of the tight-waisted jacket and a high-buttoned waistcoat with narrow lapels; it made him feel invincible. He wore it with a cream shirt and a blue silk tie when he went with Augustine to a cocktail party in Onslow Square and on to dinner at the Jacaranda Club off Walton Street. They were in a group of ten or so, only some of whom were known to Alfred. At the far end of the table sat an older man with a pale aquiline face and an air of distinguished boredom; beside him sat a woman of such perfectly presented beauty that Alfred thought she must be a film star. She looked a little like Jean Simmons but more delicate and more sophisticated. She seemed to take very little part in the conversation but sat straight in her chair, eating slowly and putting down her knife and fork between each mouthful, and occasionally turning towards one or other of her neighbours as if to listen intently to what they were saying. This movement, though slight, seemed made with her whole body rather than with her head alone, and this made Alfred wonder whether she might be a dancer, but when he had made an excuse to pass behind her chair by going to the lavatory, he came back convinced she could only be a duke's daughter, so confidently upper-class were her vowels, her voice so crystal-clear and dulcet sweet.

'I simply don't need God at all,' she said.

The subject was no surprise to Alfred, who had met several times the rumpled and slightly inebriated young man to whom she was speaking and knew that at a certain stage in the evening his thoughts tended to turn incoherently towards the Great Unknown.

'I simply don't need him,' she said, kind, amused, a duke's daughter who funnily enough had never liked chocolates.

Later, in his invincible suit, Alfred was about to ask her to dance, when the man beside her, without changing his expression of distinguished boredom, put a hand on her arm and rose to his feet; she immediately followed suit.

'You're not going?' called out a voice from halfway down the table on Alfred's side.

She smiled an apology. It was an unexpectedly wide, self-deprecating smile; it showed her perfect teeth and slightly raised her perfect eyebrows, but it also made her look as if she wanted very much to be liked.

'Do you know her?' Alfred asked Edwina, the girl sitting next to him.

Edwina shook her head and asked Augustine, who was on her other side.

'That's Babbington,' said Augustine. 'He's some kind of art dealer. But mainly he lives by organizing gambling games. I've told you about him.'

'Isn't it illegal?' said Edwina.

'He never gets caught. They're always in a different place, rather lavish private parties except that he takes a cut.'

'But the girl,' said Alfred. 'Who is the girl?'

'Lydia Starkey. He saw her in the Mile End Road. Her father had a barrow. Babbington bought her from him and sent her to a finishing school somewhere in the country to learn to be a lady. He uses her in the business a bit, to bring in the punters.'

'That's impossible,' said Edwina. 'You can't buy people. It can't be true.'

'Of course it's not true,' said Alfred. 'Augustine's a terrible liar.'

'It may not have been a barrow,' said Augustine. 'It may have been a shop selling second-hand picture frames.'

Scene at a gambling party. Somewhere outside London. A stockbroker-Tudor house, footmen in some kind of livery, plovers' eggs, champagne, too many flowers. Babbington presiding with his air of quiet distinction and controlled geniality, men with money, some of Eastern aspect, some English with high blood pressure and large cigars, pink-faced youths with over-excited voices, rather drunk (young blades mortgaging their futures), pretty girls looking bored, restrained music, too much warmth, to make up for the host's cold eyes, and slim between the dark suits the tender form of Lydia the lamb for the slaughter, the young goat tethered to lure the prowling tiger, who, bending over to offer her a cigarette from his gold case, lets his yellow eyes linger on her sacrificial neck.

Lydia's past. Alfred had glimpsed it only once.

'I have thrown off my past,' she had said, when he met her later, at some other party.

What had happened was that gambling had been legalized and had lost its allure for Babbington. He had a share in a casino somewhere, but his special hold over his clientele had gone. He had turned Lydia into a fashion model, icon of the new age, since to be possessor of an icon carries a certain cachet; but in fact that new world was not for him, its cheerful commercialism no more than its cloudy idealism. His pursuit of the strangely addictive power of knowing discreditable things about important people took him elsewhere – quite where Alfred never knew nor wanted to know. He went underground about the time of the Profumo affair, resurfaced but was never quite the same. He belonged there, in the pre-permissive age, when wickedness was wickedness, before the frontiers fell. As far as Alfred was concerned, Babbington had to be beyond some frontier, any frontier, so long as he was on the other side of it.

7

Each day they waited to see whether the fog would lift. Sometimes it did, and a still day of low sunlight and long shadows followed, though the temperatures remained below freezing. Sometimes hardly any light at all seemed to penetrate the pearl grey cloud which blanketed everything. Sometimes the cloud was white with hidden sunlight which failed to break through. There was never a breath of wind.

'I noticed when I was driving here,' said Edith, 'that there seemed to be piles of rubble dumped in front of quite a few gates into fields. Have the travellers been around again?'

'They never go away. There are about two hundred on the old railway track. There's a rumour they're going to be moved out, so people are putting up the barricades.'

'Might they not move into the old farmyard?'

'John Jarrett did padlock it once. But I think it's so near this house they wouldn't risk it.'

'John didn't mind Lydia's hippy friends.'

'Different.'

'Wouldn't it be safer if you owned it?'

'I don't want it.'

'I suppose I could buy it.'

'What on earth would you do with it?'

'I could run courses in it. Optional extras for my students, combined with a glimpse of English life outside London. Or intensive courses for foreign businessmen. We get lots of those.'

'It's all falling down. You'd have to spend a fortune.'

'The school's quite rich. And I'd have no trouble getting a loan if I needed it.'

'Are you serious?'

Edith lost her nerve.

'I don't know,' she said. 'I've only just thought of it.'

Alfred said he thought he would take the dogs for a walk. They appeared busily as soon as they heard the boot cupboard being opened. He let them out, shrugging on his thick jacket and feeling in the pocket for gloves; there being none, he shut the door behind him and returned his hands to his pockets for warmth, scrunching the hoar frost under his feet as he set off up the hill. The black dog ran heavily ahead, hampered by the ebullient terrier who was trying to hang on to his ears; the lurcher streaked past them and disappeared into the beech trees.

'Jinks!' shouted Alfred, not wanting the lurcher to find the scent of a rabbit and cut himself on the barbed wire while in hot pursuit, something which no amount of previous experience seemed to have taught him to avoid. Though his rough coat was white apart from a black patch round one eye and another on his rump, he had a completely black whippet called Nijinsky two generations back in his ancestry and seemed to have inherited his turn of speed. Nijinsky had been Lydia's dog; she had christened him not so much because of his high leaps as because when he was excited he would turn round and round in a tight circle like a dancer without ever seeming to lose his balance.

Alfred was uneasy. He felt he wanted only to live alone, follow his accustomed tracks, take the dogs for walks. He hoped Edith had been talking idly, but suspected she had not; he knew that elaborately casual tone. 'I'm thinking of leaving Johnny,' she had said; and later on, 'Derek seems to have disappeared,' and worst of all, 'They seem to think it might be something more than just bronchitis.' Which of course it was, and she knew it; it was the first appearance of the cancer which killed their mother. And he should have been there when she died; and he should have been there for the funeral. Not that she who had never wanted him to suffer the slightest pain would have wanted him to see her die; but

70

she would have liked him to have been at the funeral, because that would have been the proper thing. He felt it as a due unpaid. He had been to see her often enough when she was ill, first in hospital and then on quick visits home, cheering her with tales of his adventures in commerce, relieving his father of the sickbed duties he performed so ineptly, freeing him to shut himself up with his piano and thunder out themes for the oratorio he never finished. She had sat in a high-backed chair by the fire, coughing, wrapped in a shawl but never warm; in the afternoons her thin, grey face brightened with interest as people came and went, talking to her, tending her (because she was liked even by those who found her shyness difficult to overcome), and then exhaustion would subdue her. But she was not expected to die so quickly; no one foresaw how easily she would accept defeat. She died when Alfred and Lydia were in America. They had finished their business discussions and gone to stay with a millionaire in Arizona who had taken them on a horse trek into the desert, so that by the time the message reached Alfred the funeral was over. Lydia would have enjoyed telling her about the desert; she had been charmed by Lydia, had listened to their stories about their exploits as if to something from an *Arabian Nights'* entertainment, as indeed in retrospect they seemed.

'Leda Starelski,' someone had said. 'You know, she's famous.'

A young girl with wide eyes and long legs, a cool gaze suddenly modified by a surprisingly friendly smile. 'Some stupid agent called me that when I started modelling. My real name's Lydia Starkey. As far as I know.'

'Then we've met.'

'Yes. You stared.'

'But you're so young.'

'I've thrown off my past. It's very rejuvenating. You're staring again.'

Edwina took his arm. 'Gus is in the car.'

'If you ever feel like being stared at you know where I am.'

71

'No. I don't.'

'Ask anyone.' Because he was already becoming arrogant.
It had started with Alfred's Cakes. Edwina cooked them,
Augustine dealt with the orders and Alfred drove the delivery
van, with the name painted on the side. It was Augustine's
idea; he said everyone knew the story about King Alfred
burning the cakes, so they would remember the name. Augustine and Alfred had both left their jobs. Edwina had never
had a job because she was an heiress, but she had done a
Cordon Bleu cookery course and could afford to buy the
van. She had been to America and learnt to like American
cookies. She was consequently quite plump but comely
enough to have appealed to Augustine even before he discovered her to be an heiress. She had an explosive giggle and a
scatterbrained attitude to money which probably justified her
father's anxiety. He was a property tycoon and she was his
only daughter; his vigorous campaign to prevent her from
marrying Augustine, she being under twenty-one and legally
under his authority, involved talk of horsewhips and threats
of injunctions and much consequent publicity in the gossip
columns. This contributed to the success of Alfred's Cakes, to
which were added, as soon as premises were acquired, Alfred's
Clothes, Augustine's Books and Edwina's Objects. All this
was housed in a converted wharf further down the Chelsea
Embankment than had hitherto been considered fashionable;
outside hung a painted sign proclaiming Alfred's Emporium.
Only the addition of the coffee bar was needed to make it
what *Queen* magazine called the Fountainhead of the New
Fizz.

Edith, clearing away the breakfast (it was not one of the days
for Mrs Weeks and Mrs Jupp), thought there was one thing
about Hubert, which was that he never took offence. Alfred
had always been prone to abrupt retreats into silence, or
sudden dashes out on to the hill with the dogs. Edith knew
that, and knew that he would never subsequently refer to

whatever it was which had upset him, and that if she wanted to know she would have to wait, and then approach the matter with caution. In this case she knew already not only that he had taken fright at her idea about the farm buildings, but that he might well have resented her speaking of Lydia's hippy days in the same breath as she mentioned the current New Age travellers. She knew his views about the latter, had even been mildly amused at his vehemence in view of his own youthful experience, and should probably have remembered not to complicate the issue of the farm buildings by bringing in something extraneous and annoying. At least with Hubert, she thought, there was no need to worry about being annoying; he never seemed to mind. She supposed – putting away plates and allowing herself to think of him with affection – that he was her oldest friend, unless you counted Caroline Cornish, whom she had known longer and who was theoretically a friend but whom she had never really much liked, any more than she supposed Caroline liked her. Hubert had written helpfully of Edith's first entry into politics, but she had not met him until after she had become a Member of Parliament. He had referred in an article to her career as a school rugger champion and she had telephoned him to say that she had never been any such thing. The mistake had arisen because she had been taken under the wing of a kindly old Conservative Member called Sir Raymond Chadwick.

Whenever in those early days she had some query about Parliamentary procedure, whomever she asked, from whatever party, directed her towards Ray Chadwick. He was a self-appointed expert, a backbencher in his late sixties with no ambitions for office and a romantic love of the institution in which he found himself and whose history and traditions, intricacies and intrigues, he found wholly absorbing. He had been a Labour man in his youth, but a successful career in the grocery trade had made him a capitalist. Unlike many of his colleagues he had not been to a public school, and the joys of a male hierarchical institution came to him fresh and made his old age a happy one. On Budget Day he was always the first in his seat, dressed with old-fashioned propriety and carrying a top hat; even on ordinary Parliamentary days he wore a black jacket, a stiff wing collar and pinstriped trousers. He was a loyal party member, believing his leaders to be by and large a fine body of men. He was delighted to be consulted on questions of procedure, as he often was, by Members whose experience of the House was longer than his own; he would answer at length, giving his sources, even quoting page references in May's *Parliamentary Procedure*. If he was a bore, he was a useful one, and Edith came to like him. When one afternoon, as they sat in close conversation on a bench in the central lobby, a rather unpleasant Labour Member who tended to drink too much at lunchtime came past and sneeringly warned Edith to watch out – 'You know he's known as Randy Raymond' – Ray, who was certainly known as nothing of the kind, looked seriously upset and rose to his feet to begin a rather cumbersome protest. Edith interrupted him to say scornfully to the Labour man, 'Don't be pathetic,' adding loudly as he went on his way with a satirical wave, 'And I played centre forward in my school rugger team so you'd better watch it.'

This remark, having been overheard, was referred to on the floor of the House in jocular vein during the course of a fairly boring and ill-attended debate on the Government's failure to provide nursery education. Hubert, having nothing much else to write about that week, made some play with it. Edith telephoned him as soon as she read the article.

'Could you just drop that bit about my being a rugger player, do you think? It isn't true.'

'What a shame. How did it get about?'

'I made it up. It was nothing. A silly joke.'

'It would be nice if we could have lunch one day, if you have time, just to talk about how things are going with the ICP and so on.'

He did not ask about the story at lunch and she did not

mention it because she could see that he could make her look ridiculous. She found his attitude to politics cynical but appreciated his experience. By the end of lunch she felt that he liked her, and when later on he did ask her if she had ever played rugger the degree of sympathy with which he immediately appreciated the difficulty of being a woman in a male institution was neither too much nor too little but unexpectedly comforting; she noticed that afterwards in his articles he seemed to be unobtrusively becoming something of a personal champion. Of course, he had been a bit fat, even then. The truth was, though, that one liked people to be typical of themselves, even when this manifested itself in ways which were intrinsically irritating; just as one liked French people to be sharp and chauvinistic and Italians to be ironical and late. So she could not now truly want Hubert to be an ascetic or Alfred to be less thin-skinned. Perhaps in turn neither of them wanted her to be tactful. Alfred must know that she had never been sympathetic to Lydia's hippy phase; she felt it had diverted him from the way he was in, which might have made him rich. But he would have thought her wrong, and Lydia right.

She had wanted Lydia to like her. Alfred had brought her to tea. They came in the van and brought some cakes. Edith and Johnny had sold the house in Markham Street and moved further down the King's Road into a street where the houses, larger and better built than the Markham Street ones, were mainly held on long leases; as the leases expired the landlords were improving the houses and selling new leases for a much increased sum, so that some houses were a great deal smarter than others and the people who lived in the unregenerate houses knew that they would not be there for long. Sarah was three and a half and Edith had been to see an expensive kindergarten near Sloane Square which was favoured by several of her friends; she had been told that there was no room for Sarah because the school had become so popular that parents had to put their children's names down at birth. Edith, challenged, started a play group in her own street, asking parents to contribute what they felt they could to the expenses, and forming a management committee with the more active of the other mothers. So began the movement which spread from street to street, made her its spokeswoman and in due course propelled her on to the local council. Caroline Cornish called it too peculiar – how were people to know what their children would pick up (she meant nits, which did sometimes feature, but could be dealt with by carbolic shampoo). Caroline had married a successful stockbroker and lived in Mallord Street. She had two children and a nanny and an under-nanny and then, because it seemed that everybody was selling something, she had two shops, called Instant Bliss and Too Peculiar (her favourite phrases). Instant Bliss sold extravagantly wonderful ball dresses, the making of which Caroline herself meticulously supervised, and Too Peculiar sold clothes which Caroline bought wherever the whim led her and which she called 'kooky'. Both became fashionable with a slightly more traditional clientele than those who frequented Alfred's Emporium, though there was considerable overlap. Too Peculiar had the first open-plan changing-room in London; Princess Margaret was said to have been seen in there in her underclothes, though some said a lady-in-waiting had held up a sheet, and others said it had not been Princess Margaret at all.

Lydia was wearing a sea-blue shift and a wide-brimmed straw hat, Alfred a crumpled Mao shirt and linen trousers with a jacket slung over his shoulders which might have been a Hussars uniform. They stood on the doorstep holding the familiar red and green cake boxes. They had tea in the new cheerful kitchen with the blue and white squared linoleum floor and the white formica cupboard tops and the blue formica table where Sarah sat and ate the cakes extremely messily, clowning to Alfred as she always did. A football came soaring over the high wall at the back of the garden which they overlooked from the big kitchen window. The garden was so small that there was only room for one narrow flower bed and Sarah's sandpit, with which she was already disillusioned because the sand so soon gave way to the concrete underneath. It was on this concrete (the estate agents' particulars had called it a patio) that the football bounced, and then rebounded against the window, but without much force. Sarah, surprised and interested, wanted to go with Alfred to throw it back over the wall but Edith said she should finish her cake first.

'There's no street there,' said Lydia. 'Where has it come from?'

'It's going to be a new wing of the hospital. It used to be the old workhouse. They occasionally put people in there, people from these houses probably, before they find council flats for them.'

'They'll go to those lovely new towers, I suppose. A friend of mine tried to get a flat there, but he was told he hadn't lived in Chelsea long enough.'

Alfred tried to climb up the wall to see over it before he threw back the ball. Sarah finished her cake and got down from her chair but instead of going outside to join Alfred she went over to sit on Lydia's knee, leaning her head dreamily on to Lydia's bosom. It was not at all the sort of thing she usually did and Edith, embarrassed, suggested that she was covered in cake and should wash. Lydia, leaning her cheek on Sarah's fair head, said she didn't mind.

'Children often do this,' she said. 'What is it about me that makes them want to go to sleep?'

'I hope it doesn't mean she's going to be sick,' said Edith.

Lydia only smiled a little sadly, thus presenting to Alfred when he returned, as to Johnny when he shortly came back from the office, a picture of touching tenderness. Edith found this irritating, and thought Johnny's effusive friendliness overdone, but at the same time she was no more immune than they were to Lydia's peculiar power, which consisted not just in her beauty and at times her gaiety but in her capacity to make people feel an intimate concern for her. She had a sort of waif-like pose, sometimes maddening and never possible to take quite seriously, particularly since by the time Edith met her she was already very successful in her career, but behind it there seemed an occasional desperation, as if the pose might conceal not less need of help than she pretended but more, as if she were a child playing at being lost while having at the same time no idea where she was going. Later Edith came to see this as a dangerous enchantment, a means by which Lydia could make other people see what she herself saw, the world reflected in a distorting mirror; but by that time Edith had decided that Lydia was a destroyer.

When Alfred came back from his walk he found John Jarrett standing by the Aga in the kitchen having a cup of coffee with Edith; he had heard that Alfred had been asking for him in the pub and had called in on his way to feed his horses. He was not tamed by being inside the warm kitchen, its dresser full of Wedgwood china and assorted mugs, its two cotton-reel armchairs with their comfortable cushions; he stood as he would have stood patiently on a damp hillside waiting to make his move, steal some cattle, avenge a wrong, elope with the inn-keeper's daughter. Arthur Ashby used to call him Ishmael when he was a boy playing truant from school. ' "He will be a wild man," ' he said, quoting from Genesis. ' "His hand will be against every man, and every man's hand against him." ' The idea of John Jarrett's wildness used to please him; he said he was a throwback, might have run along the rhines with Monmouth's rebels, swung on a lonely gibbet after Judge Jeffreys' Bloody Assize. Perhaps he would have been disappointed had he known how quiet a man the boy became.

A furious barking from outside signified that Alfred's dogs had discovered John Jarrett's, which were shut in his van. Alfred called his own into the house and sent them to their cushions in the back kitchen, then he poured himself out a cup of coffee and sat on the edge of the big wooden kitchen table to drink it. The terrier reappeared and jumped lightly on to the table beside him with the evident intention of sitting on his knee. Alfred moved further on to the table so as to accommodate the dog, who settled himself on his back across Alfred's knees so that Alfred had to support him with one arm as if he were a baby. This foolish position, which was the terrier's favourite, gave rise to slow talk of dogs, to which Edith left the two men, saying she had promised to ring up Sarah in London.

'So you're a rich man, John,' said Alfred, 'having sold the farm.'

'It went to the bank mostly. Couldn't believe their luck, I shouldn't wonder. But I've got myself a bungalow the other side of the village with a decent garden to grow some vegetables and a field for a few horses. I'm still renting a field up here from the new chap, but I'll sell those horses come the spring.'

'You won't be doing so much dealing, then?'

'I've a big yard by the bungalow. I'm going to do up a few cars and such, I've always liked messing about with engines. I might get a young chap to give me a hand, make a bit of a business of it.'

'I suppose there's more money in that than in farming these days.'

'There'll be no small farms left soon. It's only the big businesses that can cope with all the paperwork, grants and that, and then they keep changing them. Suddenly it's all set-aside, thistles and ragwort, makes no sense to me. I do a bit of sawing, mind. If you get a tree down, I've got the big chainsaw, don't forget.'

'I won't. Can you find me some roe deer? One of the country magazines wants a cover photograph. They've got an article saying there's a population explosion – I don't know whether it's true.'

'In these parts it is. I can take you to a wood where you'll see three or four any day. Early or late's best.'

'Early, then? One day next week?'

Alfred's good humour was restored by this conversation. Even when he remembered as he came back into the kitchen after walking with John to his van that he had not asked him what he knew about the new owner of the farm, he could not feel that it mattered; there would be time enough. John Jarrett had about him a lack of urgency which Alfred found regenerative. His slowness was the result not of constraint but of calm; talking to him eased the way for clearer thinking when he'd gone. Alfred wished he could explain this to Edith. Edith always wanted action. An empty building seemed to her to need filling with people as soon as possible, all doing useful things and never just sitting about. But he had not minded her comparing Lydia's hippy friends, who did just sit about, with the travellers, whose idleness seemed to him destructive, because he was not nearly as sensitive about Lydia as he knew that Edith thought he was. He had changed, had accepted certain things, thought about them. He did not know how to make her understand that. It had been another self, not just a much younger one, who had sat at a restaurant table on the decisive day, reading a book, and had been surprised when he looked up to see Lydia, whom he had not seen since the time she told him he had stared at her, and who might have been expected to frequent classier eating places than his local Greek taverna, whose faithful clientele were attracted by the prices rather than the cuisine. She was with a man Alfred did not know. From where he sat he could see only her profile, half concealed by her long hair; she was looking down at the table, apparently not talking much to her companion. He did not think she had seen him, but after a time he looked up from his book to find her standing beside his table. She sat down opposite him, and said without smiling, 'Here I am.' He asked the waiter for another glass and poured her out some wine, without speaking. The man she had been with came over and without looking at Alfred said irritably to Lydia, 'Are you coming back or not?' She said, 'Not.' The man went away, paid his bill and left.

'Someone I met,' Lydia said.

In fact she had been living with him for nearly a year; he was quite a good painter.

Edith was still talking on the telephone when Alfred went through from the kitchen to the sitting-room which had been their father's study. She was sounding worried.

'You can't just not go,' she was saying.

He left her and went upstairs to change his socks which were wet. The dog followed and made himself comfortable on the bed.

'You're not allowed up here, Tommy,' said Alfred half-heartedly.

The dog's tail trembled in amiable acknowledgement. Alfred wanted to go up to the top floor and sort through the negatives which he had been putting in order for some time now and which he had almost succeeded in systematizing, but he was prevented from doing so partly by a feeling of physical discomfort as a result of having drunk too much the previous night, and partly by the thought that he ought to go downstairs again and find out whether Edith was planning to go into the village to buy the bread and vegetables they needed, and whether if so she would rather take his car, which was better than hers on the icy roads. At the same time he felt clear in his mind as to what he was going to do when he did go upstairs and sure that the reduction of the muddle of material he had there to some kind of order would make certain things about what he had been doing all this time clear to him, and so remind him how many ideas he still wanted to pursue. This certainty, and the feeling that some of these ideas were already circulating half in and half out of his consciousness, made it less important that he should get back to work immediately; there was a process already under way, and delay was more likely to feed than destroy it, so when he had changed his socks he went downstairs to find Edith. She had finished talking on the telephone and was standing by the window looking out into the dim morning.

'Robert is going to be sent to Hong Kong,' she said. 'Sarah says she won't go.'

'How long is he going for?'

'At least two years. Two years at first anyway. It's a tremendously good job. He'll be paid a fortune.'

'That's good, then, isn't it?'

'Sarah says she's not going to give up her own career, so she's going to stay in London. I've never heard anything so stupid. Not that I want them to go so far away, although I suppose they get flown back for holidays and so on, but she ought to support her husband. His firm are keen for her to go but they've said they want him whether she does or not. His boss came to lunch on Boxing Day, that's when the whole thing came up.'

'Perhaps it's all right, then, if they don't mind?'

'But it seems to me quite wrong. She doesn't need the money and he won't see enough of his children and the marriage will certainly collapse. They're both highly impatient people and quite reasonably attractive. They're bound to find other people. It's all completely unsatisfactory.'

'You've often said you don't really like Robert much.'

'I don't have to like him, Sarah does. He's a perfectly good father to the children. I don't want them to get divorced. You've no idea how horrible it is getting divorced, Alfred. It's far, far worse than anyone ever tells you. And there are the children. I only had Sarah and she was too young to know much about it, and then with Derek he wasn't there, so in one way it wasn't so bad though I did hate having to sell the house of course. How could she be so selfish?'

'She's good at her job, I suppose. They don't think the husband's job more important than the wife's these days.'

'It's a ghastly job, peddling lies to a whole lot of nincompoops. Totally unnecessary and doesn't do the least bit of good to anybody.'

'Provides jobs, I suppose.'

'I'm going to buy some bread and stuff. If she rings up again, tell her to pull herself together.'

'It's more the sort of thing she usually says to me, but I'll try. D'you want to take my car? It's better on the ice.'

'No thanks, I'm used to mine.'

As she drove off rather fast down the drive, she skidded quite considerably and hit the grass verge. Slowing down, she reasserted control over the car and turned on the radio; the music was stormy and discordant. Dissatisfied, she turned it off and thought about Sarah. Sarah was efficient and well-organized. If she decided not to go with Robert to Hong Kong, she presumably knew what she was doing. But Alfred, the house, the encounter with Johnny and Hermione, had combined to revive Edith's memories. It had been years since she had thought about her divorce from Johnny, Sarah's father, and suddenly the other night she had found herself feeling something approaching remorse for her part in it. It was absurd, after so long. She had no wish to remember how she had sat with her parents in the drawing-room in the summer, the windows open to the evening air, a violet-tinged dusk quietly claiming the day, blackbirds making their sharp alarm calls in the garden, a thrush singing on the weeping ash, rooks beginning to settle in the tall limes, and had said, 'He's drunk when he gets home. He stops at the pub and comes home drunk. He threw an electric fire into the bath when I was in it.'

Her mother's face turned completely white. 'But it could have killed you.'

'I jumped out. I slipped and hit my head on the edge of the door.' She lifted her hair to show the bruise.

Her mother said quite faintly. 'We must see you get the best possible legal advice.'

It was her father who protested, though he did it, as so often, in the name of her mother. 'You don't know what this means to your mother.' How he talked; every time he slowed down a new wave of emotion seemed to sweep over him. 'It meant so much to her, your marriage. You don't understand, these things matter. You don't know anything about the world.'

Darkness took possession of the world outside the window. Janet Ashby rose silently to turn on the lights. Later she shut the windows and drew the curtains, then sat down again on an upright chair, her hands clasped in front of her, her back straight, her face as white and shocked as before.

'A man drinks when he's unhappy,' her father said. 'Have you thought that he might feel upset because you're so busy with the schools, and now with the council? Has it got worse since you decided to stand for the council? Have you been thoughtless?'

'It's gone too far. I've told him I'm leaving him.'

'If you leave his house, you put yourself in the wrong. You have to think of that. You haven't thought of the consequences. What about people round here? Johnny's family are respected, they mean something. You don't understand all that. We have brought you up to be too unworldly. No one can afford to ignore these things.'

'What things?' she had said, unwisely because she knew what was coming.

'Social matters. It meant a great deal to your mother, your marriage. It took you into the world she came from. She made a great sacrifice when she married me. She came from a county family, my father was a shoemaker.'

'No one thinks like that these days.'

'If they don't, they should. The whole structure of English life depends on a proper understanding of these things. It's why we are a stable society. If young people in London think they can cast off all the conventions, they're wrong.'

'You're not thinking of me. You're saying I've got to put up with anything so that you and Mummy can mix with the county.'

'Of course I'm not saying that. You know perfectly well we don't entertain. Our life is my music. I'm simply saying that as Johnny's wife you are somebody. If you divorce him you will be a nobody again.'

'I don't want to be somebody. Not that sort of somebody, anyway.'

84

'Perhaps you should have thought of that when you married him.' And this was her father, who was never happier than when accompanying her while she sang, who encouraged her enthusiasms, laughed at her frankness, applauded her school successes; this angry, hurt and, in some odd way, frightened man.

Eventually Edith had said she must go to bed. Her father, sunk in his chair, had put his hand over his eyes. Her mother had come with her to the drawing-room door and put a hand on her arm.

'It will be all right. We'll see that it's all right.'

Edith kissed her quickly and said, 'Sleep. We all need sleep.'

She did not sleep herself. Early in the morning her father appeared in her bedroom in his dressing-gown, which was too small for him because he was beginning to get fat. With one hand he awkwardly held together the front vent in his sagging pyjama trousers; his face was swollen with insomnia and tears.

'You mustn't be unhappy. We'll help you. We'll look after you.' The embrace, his face damp with tears and his breath unhealthy, then his shambling retreat from the room, shoulders bent like an old man; was he not exaggerating a little?

There were no more reproaches. The divorce took its acrimonious course and afterwards Edith spent a good deal of time with her parents, especially during Sarah's school holidays. She was grateful for her mother's support but the distance between them did not diminish. The truth was that her mother maddened her, by her passivity, her meekness, her moral certainties, her dedication to her husband. That was no life for anyone, Edith thought. And yet for her mother it was clearly the only life for a woman. As for her father, relations were superficially the same as ever, but she had let him down, and there it was.

Now, years later, driving along the icy road towards the village, Edith thought how being so much closer to Sarah than her mother had ever been to her she must be right to try to interfere. Even in her own case she did wonder why her mother had not made more effort to discuss things with her. But then, what difference would it have made? And had not she herself made her mother believe that Johnny was a would-be murderer? It was true that he had called in at the pub on his way home, and that when he came into the bathroom he was carrying the two-bar electric fire which they usually had in their bedroom. He had stopped at the electrician's to collect it; it had had to have one of the elements replaced. When she had shouted from the bathroom that she was getting ready to go out because she had a meeting, he had come straight in with the fire under his arm to expostulate angrily, and when she answered in kind, he became incoherent, suddenly dropped the fire into the end of the bath where her feet were and stamped out of the room. It gave her a fright of course, and made her even angrier, but it was not attempted murder. Why had her mother not asked whether the fire was plugged in? And anyway, whoever told the truth when they were talking about marital conflict? But she had always meant to be the sort of person who did tell the truth. So now, years later, she resented being made to think about things she didn't want to think about, being made to feel mean-spirited, vengeful, worst of all mistaken.

'Damn Sarah,' said Edith, banging the steering-wheel with both hands.

8

Alfred was looking for some pictures which might illustrate a guide-book about the Mendips. Mr and Mrs Sainty, who were writing the book, were both retired school teachers, expert in local history; they had asked Alfred for some photographs, correctly assuming that he would have plenty to choose from. He had a storage system for his negatives and he or Beryl, the not particularly efficient secretary who came in once a week, could usually find what was required when asked for prints, but he had not sorted through it for some time and the Saintys' interest had stimulated him to begin to do so. The attic bedrooms were now as a result festooned with prints, some old and yellowing, others new, since he could not always resist the temptation to stick an old negative under the enlarger lamp and then, dipping the blank sheet in the developer tray, watch the captured moment materialize, as if memory could recreate the light which had first made it manifest, and having done so choose where to freeze it, at what point to fix the collector's pin through the butterfly instant, by lifting the dripping paper from the dish and hanging it up to dry. So, looking for scenes for the Saintys, he surveyed his images of the familiar hills and plateaux and vast skies but not of the valley behind the house, for though he had records of that in every season he did not want people to find it who did not already know and love it. He himself liked best the pictures of great clouds lowering over hedges blown sideways by the prevailing winds, a glint of light perhaps on water from a flooded stream, and the trees printed in dark to dramatize them, but thinking the Saintys might favour sunnier scenes he looked at well-set villages too, and farms and manor houses, churches, towers, follies and ruins.

The Saintys knew about houses that had crumbled, and families that had vanished. They had told Alfred about the three generations of the Barwell family who had lived at the house beyond his own: how they had owned mines and driven to church in a phaeton and had a daughter who married the steward of one of the big local estates; and how the son had died in the Crimean War and why their memorials were not in the village church but in the church four miles away where the mother's family had come from; and how when no buyer could be found for the grandiose and inconvenient Victorian house, it had been pulled down so that such pieces of the fabric as had any value could be sold to try and ward off bankruptcy; and how the flagstones were to be found in a nearby dairy, and one of the heavy carved stone fireplaces in a house the other side of the Mendips and the dressed stone from the window frames in a farmhouse towards Cheddar, dispersed but not lost.

In Alfred's indexing system the Mendips appeared under their own name but also under 'Hills', and when he investigated 'Hills' he found some pictures of the High Atlas which properly belonged under 'Mountains', but equally could be categorized as 'Travel' and so should come under the sub-heading 'Morocco'; then when he looked at 'Morocco' he found some pictures of whirling dervishes which Beryl had wrongly included there when they should have been under 'Sudan' and which should certainly be cross-referenced to 'Movement', which was one of the most interesting sections and in the course of the re-examination of which he had almost covered the walls and most of the furniture in one of the attic bedrooms with prints. When he went in to see if there were any whirling dervishes there already, he looked out of the window to see whether Edith's car was back and saw a shiny new vehicle of racy aspect, something like a toy jeep, parked by the farmyard. A man in a Barbour jacket and a tweed cap appeared to be inspecting the buildings. Alfred recognized Charles Warburton, but hoped Edith would come back before he needed to go down himself.

Turning away from the window, he came face to face with a whirling figure pinned to a tall mirror, but it was not a dervish, it was Lydia, blissful and uplifted in drifts of white chiffon. It came from his first fashion series; Lydia had been so giddy that she had fallen over as soon as the picture was taken. It had been in the first year after she had come to live with him, and they had recently been to France for a few days, taking the car on the aeroplane from Lydd to Le Touquet. One afternoon after a good lunch they found themselves near something which announced itself as the National Stud, so they wandered into the stables of the fine château and looked at the horses, sturdy percherons and Normandy cobs and beautiful mad-eyed race-horses bred for speed. One of these last had been led outside, dancing dangerously on the cobbles as they sat in the sun and watched.

Alfred said, 'She has eyes like yours.'

Lydia jumped up and ran very fast across the mown grass, leapt over a low wooden fence into the park, stumbled and rolled over to lie spreadeagled on her back. Alfred, long-legged, stepped over the fence to sit beside her.

'I thought as much,' he said.

She took one of his hands and said, 'I'm so happy.'

She had given him a Rolleiflex camera some time before. He had become interested in photography because he liked talking to her friend Stanley when he went to his studio to meet her. He sometimes filled in as Stanley's assistant, and when he had his own camera he went to evening classes to learn more about technique. Lydia thought this funny, but Alfred said if everyone was going to photograph her he might as well do so too. In fact he had found a way of doing what he most liked doing, which was simply looking at things. Introduced to editors by Lydia, he did some fashion photography but soon moved to other subjects. First however he did his running and jumping pictures of Lydia, which were enormously successful, and appeared in magazines all over the world. The fashion designers eventually complained that no one could see the clothes properly, but in the meantime his enthusiasm had left him. He disliked the way Lydia's beauty was used, as if she were a dress-maker's dummy which happened to breathe; he hated to see her pinned and poked and prinked by over-made-up middle-aged women with cigarettes in their mouths who talked to each other across her and only spoke to her to issue orders, and the comments of all the photographers except Stanley seemed to him carelessly offensive. When he said something of this to Lydia, she dismissed it at once, saying she did it for the money, cared nothing for any of them and thought of other things while they manipulated her. Alfred forbore to point out that a prostitute might have said the same, and decided to have nothing more to do with her modelling work for fear of making her angry by his possessiveness. He was learning new strategies of love, having already progressed some way beyond the preliminary skirmishes in which each had wanted the other to be the first to signify submission. Either his pride or some correct intuition as to Lydia's character had made him feel that he must be cautious; so when they made love and he longed to say, 'I love you,' he only said, 'I want you'; and when he finally said, 'I think I may be falling in love with you,' it was long after he could first truthfully have told her he adored her. She said, 'Never rely on me, never, never.' He duly promised. He meant to love her well; she deserved and demanded it. He felt he could achieve a masterpiece of loving.

'I'd never have thought it of you,' Augustine said. 'Sticking to one woman at your age, it's ridiculous.'

Augustine by this time had grown tired of Edwina, with whom he was nevertheless inextricably involved financially. The business of Alfred's Emporium, founded on Edwina's original investment and managed almost entirely by Augustine, was a success. Alfred, whose business acumen was very much less than Augustine's, contributed only the verdicts of his visual sense. He had a more or less absolute fiat over the choice of objects in Edwina's shop, which from dealing purely in junk and bric-à-brac had moved on to more serious antiques and works of art, in most of which some element of fantasy remained, whether in the Gothic furniture or the Mannerist paintings. To Alfred's annoyance Lydia once conveyed to him a message from Babbington. 'That young man has an eye,' he had said. 'I'll give him a job any time he wants it.' Alfred told her to tell him to get stuffed; Lydia giggled but probably modified the reply.

The design of the coffee bar, which was more like a Victorian public house than the Spanish or Italian imitations still then in vogue among its competitors, also reflected Alfred's taste. The clothes shop meanwhile continued to express a kind of romantic anarchy, but success meant the prices could be increased and so the clothes could be better made (they had had an early tendency to fall apart). Augustine insisted that Alfred and Lydia should wear them whenever possible; they had become a fashionable pair, conferring favour by their mere presence. This aspect of their life together seemed to Alfred a highly enjoyable joke. He could not think of it as having anything very much to do with him; it seemed an act which he and Lydia had had created for them by other people's expectations and which they consented to perform because it was all part of the celebratory atmosphere of the time. When he was alone, he felt himself anonymous again, that same retiring character of whose reserve his school reports used to complain. When he was with Lydia, he was emboldened, enchanted, not quite himself. Augustine exploited their social status wherever he could to feed the success of Alfred's Emporium; he began negotiations for licensing agreements with chain stores not only in London but soon in America and then in Japan. As he became ever more preoccupied with these schemes, so he gave less and less time to Edwina, to whom he had never anyway been particularly kind; she began to drink and shout, and as Alfred had a fastidious horror of drunken, shouting women, he avoided her rather than trying to make peace. Occasionally he would expostulate to Augustine, who would only groan and agree that he was a shit.

'I ought to have been queer. God how I keep hoping. They just don't know how lucky they are. Sex without responsibility, the more the better and no harm done, every man's dream.'

Charles Warburton stood in front of the fire looking round the room with evident pleasure.

'How can I get my house to look like this? This room's perfect, just as it should be. What can I do? You've seen that room of mine. It's all wrong.'

'It's very pretty,' said Edith. 'It just needs living in.'

'There's too much décor. All my wives become decorators, then they feel so guilty about leaving me they redecorate my house from top to toe before they go. I wish they wouldn't.'

'Are there many of them?'

'Three. I adore them all. They get sick of me because I spend all my time playing various ridiculous games and not enough time with them. They're quite right, it's ridiculous at my age.'

'What sort of games?'

'I'm off to St Moritz next week to do the Cresta Run. I've done it every year since I was twenty. D'you ski at all, either of you?'

Edith and Alfred said they had never skied.

'What about hunting? Quite fun round here, I believe. Mendip Farmers isn't it? Not real hunting country, though. You probably shoot,' he said to Alfred.

'Not really,' said Alfred. 'More whisky?'

Charles Warburton had lived in Spain, helping to run a polo club. There was wonderful partridge shooting there, he said. And he had shot quail in Morocco and wildfowl on the Chesapeake Bay.

'And tigers?' said Edith helpfully.

'Never even seen one. Wouldn't shoot it anyway, wonderful creatures. Not that one would be allowed to nowadays although I believe there were more about when they were preserved for big-game shooting than nowadays when they're poached to near-extinction for the Chinese market. But tell me, how d'you like your Saab?'

'Very much.'

'I must show you my latest toy, it's outside. It's just the thing for these parts.'

The telephone happening to ring just as he was leaving, only Edith walked out to his car with him. It made her laugh, because it looked like an overgrown toy jeep such as might have given pleasure to her grandson. Charles Warburton seemed pleased by her amusement.

'I can't tell you what fun they are,' he said. 'Listen, I can see your brother's a bit of an intellectual, so I didn't mention that little scheme we just touched on the other day. He won't like this particular sport at first, but he'll come round to it in the end because it's all harmless, just good fun. Come and meet me at the pub tomorrow and I'll take you for a spin.'

'I'll meet you at the pub. I'm not sure about the spin.'

'You'll love it. We can do something, you know, you and I, with that old farmyard. I'll tell you more about it tomorrow. Twelve-ish?'

Italy. How well she had done, Beryl. He had far too many photographs of Italy, and from the bundles of big brown envelopes and the folders held together with elastic bands she seemed to be at least halfway towards creating an orderly system, neatly boxed on the attic floor. There were enough bigger prints pinned up at random, some yellowing and curled up at the edges, to bring back to him the place where he had lived, in the hills north of Siena. Requests for romantic Italian landscapes came in quite often; he really ought to dig out some more. Then there were street scenes, and bar scenes, and literally hundreds of pictures of grape-picking and wine-making and Palli and Milanesi pruning the olives. He had many portraits of Palli too, the archetypal peasant cultivator, looking sometimes wise and ancient and sometimes cunning and suspicious and sometimes wonderfully pleased with himself. And then, surprisingly, Edith and Derek, walking up the hill through the olives towards the house.

Alfred had not thought about Derek, Edith's second husband, for a long time. He had never much liked him, but since he had not met him until after the marriage there was no point in letting Edith see that. In fact he had made a great effort to prevent her doing so. She had brought him to stay in Italy soon after they married, with Sarah. He had to admit that Derek had always behaved admirably to Sarah. Alfred knew, because she had often referred to it afterwards, that Edith considered the visit a great success. She had said more than once how relieved she had been that Alfred had got on so well with Derek. It had been June and everything about the farmhouse had been at its most satisfactory. It stood four-square on the hillside above the descending vineyards and olive groves and patches of rough woodland, facing an immensity of similar hills and valleys reaching as far as the distant mountains. In the morning there were the loud liquid whistles of the golden orioles in the white mulberry tree and the slow scratching of Palli's hoe in the dry earth; in the evening the nightingales which had been singing most of the day sang on into the darkness as the fireflies pricked the velvet dark below the terrace. Of course Edith was happy. How could she be anything else? All the same Alfred was left with an uncomfortable feeling that perhaps he had been avoiding the issue under the pretence of being kind. Should he not have dropped some kind of hint? It was so obvious to him that Derek was a crook. He was jolly, amusing, friendly, and a bit of a crook. In retrospect Alfred blamed himself for having over-estimated Edith's degree of sophistication. He had thought she must have recognized this truth about Derek and decided to overlook it; she had always liked people who made her laugh.

Derek took them to lunch with a friend of his who had settled not far away on the outskirts of a village quite close to Siena. 'He's a clever fellow, Martin, made a fortune out of lavatory brushes or something. He's having a so-called tax break. In fact he'll make another fortune buying ruined farmhouses and doing them up to sell to the English. He's absolutely in with the local mafia.' There had been delicious food spread out on a shady terrace. The other people were all English, most of them retired. The vicar of the English church in Florence, a willowy young man with an old-fashioned air who came over once a month to conduct a service in the tiny English church in Siena, spoke of a charity which looked after the needs of elderly English nannies who had been working for Italian families when the war broke out and had somehow never managed to get back home. 'We're getting up a jumble sale,' he said to Alfred. 'Do come, you'd adore it.' Their hostess explained that Angelina and Antonio, her couple, were wonderful people, so simple and at the same time so independent – 'One feels there's something quite primitive – in the best sense, I mean – you know, close to the heart of things.' She was a short person in a flowery dress which consorted badly with her rubicund complexion. 'Everyone who was in the regiment with Martin drinks,' she said. 'But then I was in the Consular service and I drink too.' She laughed heartily.

'Don't we all?' said Alfred, laughing too.

Sarah's small hand suddenly slipped into his. 'We can walk round the garden,' she said. 'I asked.'

As they walked away, Alfred asked, 'How did you know I needed rescuing?'

'Your laugh.'

'A bit false?'

'Ha ha ha ha ha ha.'

'For Heaven's sake, they'll hear. It can't have been as bad as that.'

'Worse, worse, worse.' She ran ahead of him, skirted a bed

of red begonias edged with salvias and climbed over a fence into a vineyard. 'Now we're safe.' She picked up a stone and threw it on to the tangled grass and herbs growing at the side of the vineyard; then went and sat down where she had thrown it. 'No snakes.'

Alfred sat beside her and said, 'Derek laughs a lot.'

'Yes, but he always means it. He doesn't laugh so much at home, just when there are other people. Especially people he was in the regiment with. They all have a lot of jokes, especially about how Derek used to take things from the quartermaster's stores and sell them to the Germans.'

'Surely not.'

'Yes. When they were in Germany. Not in the war, I don't think. There was this camp and Derek had this arrangement with the quartermaster. But Mummy says it was all a joke and that anyway he was very brave in the war and won a medal. His friends aren't usually like those people at lunch.'

'Didn't you like them?'

'I was mainly just eating my lunch. But I could see you didn't like them.'

'I didn't know there were such people. I don't like to think of them living in Italy. Which is extremely stupid of me because they have just as much right to do so as I have.'

'Perhaps they're only like that when they're with their friends,' said Sarah judiciously. 'Like Derek laughing. I sometimes say quite silly things when I'm with my friends. I don't mean them really, I'm just being silly. Do you do that sometimes?'

'I suppose so. Or I did, anyway. I haven't seen much of my old friends recently. I went away. And then I found I was doing quite a lot of work here because of one particular magazine that liked my black and white landscapes and was very good at printing them, so I thought I could live here for a bit. The houses were so amazingly cheap because the people who used to live in them weren't cultivating the land any more. They went to live in the towns because they could make more money there working in factories.'

'Not so nice, though.'

'They don't seem to have noticed that yet. Perhaps they will. Anyway, I suppose the people I used to see a lot of in London don't know where I live.'

'You could send them postcards.'

It transpired that Derek had been in Italy during the war, had indeed been decorated after the Anzio landings and had then fought his way north. 'We did plenty of damage round here,' he said cheerfully. 'Bombed Poggibonsi silly.' But he talked at length to Palli in bad Italian to their evident mutual amusement and was delighted when Palli brought to show him a photograph of his brother who had been sent to fight on the Russian front and had taken one look and come straight home. Six weeks it had taken him, walking most of the way over the mountains, a home-loving man. 'There's a civilized nation for you,' said Derek approvingly.

Derek taught Sarah to play chess and when he allowed her to win took her up into the village to reward her with ice-cream. Some Dutch people who had rebuilt a ruined house with a big barn which had a paved threshing floor in front of it pinned up a notice in the village asking everyone to come and celebrate the completion of the work. Derek overcame Alfred's reluctance and insisted that they should go. An elderly lady in black sat at an upright piano in the pinkish light of dusk; supported by a violinist and a viola player, both of her own generation and of equally serious aspect, she played with tireless dedication tunes from operettas, slow waltzes, foxtrots, and a particularly individual kind of rag-time, until darkness fell and oil lamps were brought out so that the musicians could read the music. Derek danced with the grocer's stately wife, Sarah hopped about happily with the son of the house, a cadaverous thirty-year-old who told her that by the time she was grown-up he intended to be living on the moon; the pretty greengrocer's wife told Alfred he danced very well for a poet (he did not deny either imputation), while Edith gyrated slowly with the Communist mayor, saved by the language barrier from anything more than polite smiles. The Dutch host turned out to be among other things an importer of wine. Derek immediately entered into complicated negotiations with him which entailed much tasting of Chianti in the days which followed.

'Derek loves a deal,' Edith said.

'Why does Charles Warburton remind me slightly of Derek?' asked Alfred. 'Is it the way he talks?'

'The yellow jersey, I expect. Derek had one just like that. Or perhaps its the jolliness. Do you remember when Derek and I came to stay with you in Italy, with Sarah? It was the nicest holiday I've ever had, I think.'

'What happened to all those demijohns of wine Derek bought?'

'It didn't travel. And it was a tremendous bore to bottle. I think Derek managed to get rid of it to some rather doubtful restaurant at a large loss.'

'Not one of his more successful schemes.'

'Poor Derek. Go back to your filing or whatever it is you're doing. I'm going to finish rewriting this brochure, and then shall I make some supper? I'll give you a shout when it's ready.'

She did not want to talk about Charles Warburton; she wanted to find out exactly what his scheme for the farmyard was before Alfred knew anything about it. She sat down in front of the fire and ran her eye quickly over the brochure. She changed a word or two, added the odd detail, and wrote on it, 'Rose, have a look at this, it seems quite adequate to me.'

Derek would have said that Rose Brown was not exactly a ball of fire, which was true, but what would Alfred want with a ball of fire? Rose would do very well for Alfred and the farm buildings would be just the place for the school's country extension; all Edith had to do was to be patient while Alfred came round to the idea. He might even become enthusiastic. It was so much easier to work with enthusiasts, even when they were not always right. The good thing about politics had been the enthusiasm of her supporters. And of Derek, of course. She would never have got into Parliament but for Derek. He had come to see her about refuse collection. He used to tell people they fell in love over the dustbins. She was still a councillor despite being a Parliamentary candidate in another constituency, and there had been a dustmen's strike; the pavements were spilling over with ill-wrapped bundles of rotting rubbish and there were vociferous complaints. Derek had written the council several letters of advice on how to deal with the unions and finally came round one evening to express his views in person to the councillor in whose ward he lived.

'I'm awfully sorry to bother you,' he said, standing on the doorstep in his clean and cheerful way, wearing his canary-yellow pullover with a tweed jacket over it. 'I wonder if I might have a word with your husband. I am right in thinking he's on the council aren't I?'

He was unembarrassed when she explained his mistake. 'Just shows one never looks at those election leaflets. I did vote for you, but only on the spur of the moment when I saw there was an Independent candidate and I thought anything was better than that awful shit Dodds who lives next to me and lets his foul cat use my window box as a lavatory.'

He followed her into the house with the slightly rolling walk which was the result of his having lost two toes through frostbite in the Italian campaign. Sarah appeared in her dressing-gown and perched on the arm of her mother's chair. Delighted, he set out to charm them both.

He worked in public relations, was well paid and in his element. He had a way of saying shocking things without giving offence, which was odd because it was not as if he did not mean them. 'Wars are splendid things,' he would say.

'Bring out the best in people, always have. I owe everything to the war. I'd never have thought of going into the army if I hadn't been called up. Best years of my life. Wouldn't have met the people I've met, wouldn't have had half so much fun, wouldn't have got my present job. All through the old-boy network. Corrupt? Of course it's corrupt. Everywhere's corrupt. Makes the wheels go round. Mind you, you've got to stick to your local variety, like religion. No use offering a big building contract to someone at the bar of Whites, as if you were in Palermo. They'd think you were out of your mind. But you can see what you can do about a job for their ne'er-do-well son. Or arrange a lunch for them to meet someone they want to meet for some reason of their own. Little things, you know, little favours requiring other little favours in return. Call it corruption if you like, but I don't know where we'd be without it.' He pre-empted criticism by cheerfully over-stating it. 'I'm a fixer,' he would say. 'An ancient and honourable profession. Well, half honourable, anyway.'

He simply took over her life. She had been nursing her North London constituency for a year or so and, though she still enjoyed it, she thought that before long she might need to think about earning some money. Both her parents had recently died; her father had not long survived her mother, not so much because his health had failed as because he believed his life to be over and so succumbed to a bout of influenza. Edith had been left more than half of what money they had, because the house had been left to Alfred. Johnny, under the terms of the divorce settlement, gave her no alimony but allowed her to keep the house and contributed quite generously towards Sarah's expenses. Edith had had a morning job during the school terms, working for the Red Cross, but she had felt she should give this up when she took up politics, because otherwise she might not have enough time to give to Sarah. A general election was unlikely to be long delayed, and after it she thought she might honourably retire. Derek had other plans for her. He would breeze into the house with small presents of flowers or food, accept a whisky and soda and settle down to amuse both mother and daughter. Having quickly succeeded in this aim, since they found his visits invariably cheering, he moved on to advice, first of all sorting out Sarah's difficulties with a particular teacher at her school by pouring such scorn on the poor woman's alleged appearance, intellectual capacity and social provenance that Sarah lost all fear and, scorning to seek this diminished creature's approval, in no time won it. As for Edith, Derek decided she should marry again.

'You could have anything. Money, power, a great house, an art collection, anything you fancy. Use your assets. You're good-looking, charming, intelligent, sexy, one adorable daughter, you could have anybody.'

'Rubbish. That's not my sort of thing at all. Besides, where would I find these fascinating men?'

'I'll introduce you to them. Anyone you like. Prime ministers? Royalty? The Shah of Persia? No, really, between you and me he's getting bored with Soraya. Why not?'

'You must be trying to shock me. You do shock me. I don't know why I don't seem to mind being shocked. I suppose I don't believe you.'

'What about a nice Conservative peer, minor post in the Government, good place in the North, lots of money from coal, bit of a womanizer, but you could cope with that, first-rate shot . . .'

He dodged the cushion she threw at him but did ask her to dinner. He lived in a small clean characterless flat in an expensive block, but gave good dinner parties in a private room above a restaurant. Edith enjoyed herself greatly and when the Conservative peer subsequently asked her to go to the theatre with him she accepted on condition that anything Derek might have told him about her being in search of romance was untrue. Even so the evening ended in an undignified tussle, and the next day she told Derek it would not do.

'If I want a lover I'll find one for myself. I want to lead my own life not some man's. I've just got rid of one husband and I don't want another, especially not Lord Inman. And above all I don't want to be a pawn in some private game of yours.'

He said quite fiercely, 'I don't want you to be a pawn, I want you to be a queen.'

'That's just stupid.'

'Yes,' he sighed, not meeting her eye, rebuked, downcast, all bombast fled. 'I see that.' Deflated, he looked desolate.

'Well, but Derek,' she said more gently, 'it's insane, don't you see?'

'Oh, my dear girl,' he said sadly. 'What is sane in this world of madness?'

Edith, suddenly wanting to comfort him, said, 'Why don't I give a dinner party for you this time? I'll introduce you to just the woman for you.'

'She won't like me. They never do. Unless they're drunk.'

'She might be drunk, who knows? She's just left her husband. She may be in a wild mood. I haven't seen much of her lately, but I've been meaning to ask her round.'

Caroline Cornish, duly invited, had changed since Edith had last seen her. She was dressed as a Moroccan gypsy and had become a vegetarian. Derek, undaunted, dug up out of his apparently limitless acquaintance old Charley Cornish of the Queen's Dragoon Guards who had been part of the British Army of the Rhine in the late fifties, and Caroline, whose uncle he was, was amazed to hear that he had been responsible for covering a small hillock with coal, causing it to be whitewashed ('had to keep the men busy somehow') and then receiving payment for what looked like an immense heap of coal from the commander of the incoming regiment.

'Uncle Charley?' said Caroline. 'I always thought he was the soul of honour.'

'He was. He had gambling debts. As a man of honour he had to discharge them somehow.'

Later, from the other end of the table, Edith overheard Derek claiming to come of an Irish Army family.

'My father, my grandfather, his father, all the best soldiers in the British army came from Southern Ireland.'

He had told Edith that his father was a vet in County Cork, who had lost a lot of money on a patient in the Irish Derby, and so the family had moved rather hurriedly to Kilkenny. Meeting her questioning glance, Derek rolled his eyes comically, but turning back was soon swimming valiantly though quite out of his depth in a conversation about the mystic meaning of the maze. Edith went on talking to her neighbour, the friendly solicitor with whom she sometimes sang in an amateur choir. The other couple at the dinner party were architects who worked together and whom she liked. Caroline said as she left, 'You're so good, becoming serious, I mean a local councillor and everything. I couldn't do that. I couldn't become part of the system. I'm going to settle my finances with James – he's being an absolute shit, just because he put up the money for Instant Bliss when I did all the work – and then I'm getting out of London. I say I adore your bouncy friend, he's so funny, does he really know all those people he says he does?'

It was late by the time everyone left. Edith, pleased by the success of her dinner party, put on the Beatles' *Rubber Soul* and began slowly to clear up. Sarah was staying with a school friend for the night so Edith turned the sound up and sang along quite loudly. 'I'm looking through you. / Where did you go?' She had played that tune a lot when she was making up her mind to leave Johnny and it had brought on a pleasant melancholy much to be preferred to the resentment and guilt which had also assailed her.

Halfway through the record, the doorbell rang. It was Derek, slightly shame-faced.

'I thought you took Caroline home.'

'Posted her in and ran for it. Awfully sorry. I'll help you clear up.'

They ended in bed. He was an enthusiastic lover, and quite noisy. Even while she told herself that this was not really what she liked she found that his shouts – for such they were, much as if he were a spectator at a football match – made her laugh and then gasp and then forget herself in sensations which Johnny's less robust caresses had never aroused. She slept, and when much later she heard him moving around in order to dress and leave she smiled and murmured, 'Wonderful,' before going back to sleep.

Later he said, 'I suppose if you won't let me make you a famous hostess you'll have to go on with your politics. I'd better run your campaign.' Later still, Edith read in an *Evening Standard* article headed 'Drop-out Wives' that Caroline Cornish, ex-débutante, ex-wife of well-connected stockbroker, had left London to join a commune in North Wales.

9

Edith gripped the top of the windscreen in front of her as the jeep bounced and rattled up the stony track, skidding sideways from time to time and then with an extra roar of the already noisy engine lurching forward again.

'What about not going much further?' said Edith faintly. 'It can't be doing much good to our spines.'

'Terrific, isn't it?' shouted Charles. 'Hold on. Here comes the crunch.'

He changed gear and hurled the vehicle at an apparently vertical wall of frozen mud and rock.

'Hey up! Up she goes,' he shouted.

'Stop!' shrieked Edith.

'Get up there, here we go,' yelled Charles. 'Ha, ha, done it, what did I tell you? Change legs at the top, what? And down the other side. Better than hunting over banks in Ireland, what?'

'Oh no, not down,' said Edith. 'Please not down.'

'Vroom, vroom!' shouted Charles. 'This is the life!'

They hit the level ground with a crash and accelerated over the even turf.

'How's that?' shouted Charles.

Edith, overwhelmed by relief, mirth and exhilaration, shouted back 'Terrific!'

'I knew you'd enjoy it,' he said, delighted.

'It's so stupid . . .' she began, but stopped. He could not hear, anyway. She had been going to say, '. . . at my age,' but realized he was little younger and might resent being reminded of it. He was young at heart, or to put it another way completely childish. She could not wipe the smile off her face, rocketing across the fields; she had always had a weakness for childish people.

'Ridiculous,' she said. 'It's completely ridiculous.'

She was still laughing when he slammed on the brakes and skidded to a stop in front of his own house.

'Come in and have a quick snifter and then I'll drive you back to your own car.' He preceded her into the house, throwing open doors and cupboards and scattering scarf and cap and coat with the satisfied air of one who has a good day's work behind him. 'Now that track we've just come up,' he said, 'has got to be reclassified. It's got to be a Boat and not a Rupp.'

'What can you mean?' asked Edith, accepting the glass he held out to her.

'Cherry brandy OK? A Boat is a Byway Open to All Traffic and a Rupp is a Road Used as a Public Path, which may be a footpath or a bridleway. Wildlife and Countryside Act 1981, Section 54. Nothing I don't know about such matters.'

'Oh,' said Edith. 'But why?'

'Because, my dear, once you get into off-road motor sport these things become of vital import.' He put down his glass on a table and threw himself energetically into an armchair, stretching his long legs in front of him. 'Let me explain. These brilliant little vehicles need fields and tracks to buzz about on. Farmers and other landowners and people who hunt or shoot or walk their dogs or ride their horses don't necessarily like this. Under the provisions of the Act local authorities are supposed to classify all public byways. Their only criterion is previous use. So if you can get enough old crones to creep from their chimney corners and swear that they never in all their born days did see a four-wheeled vehicle on this or that track, it cannot be classified as a Boat. It may even be reclassified as a Rupp when it's been a Boat before. You see the fun ahead.'

'But surely that track's on your own land. No one can stop you driving along it, can they?'

'The plot thickens. I want other people to be able to drive

along it too. This is what I wanted to talk to you about. There's a jolly club that likes to drive around here, they call themselves the Trailblazers and they mostly come from Bristol. They're mad enthusiasts for these little machines. You'd laugh if you saw them. They're mostly accountants and things like that and they tog themselves up in racing kit and roar about the countryside getting covered in mud like so many Mr Toads.'

'You want to have them here?' said Edith doubtfully.

'Not all the time, obviously. But it would be something to do with this totally unproductive land I've got. They'd pay well, they're desperate for places to go. And besides it would be quite fun. My idea would be to turn that old stockyard opposite your brother's house into a sort of clubhouse from which the tracks would radiate. I know your brother has a covenant on it but it seems to me that as long as we limit these events to a few times a year it would be perfectly acceptable, an asset in fact.'

'I'd thought of something rather different,' said Edith.

'I know, your language courses, exactly. Why don't you and I go into partnership? When it's not in use for my Trailblazers, your foreign students move in. And vice versa. Your brother's an aesthete, I spotted that as soon as I met him. That's fine. Each to his last and so on. I also know he's quite often away. Oh yes, I've had my spies out. So why not fix weekend meetings at times of the year when he's away? Simple. And nice quiet students when he's there. What about it? Breathe a bit of life into the place, wouldn't it?'

'I'd have to think. All that bouncing has stupefied my reasoning powers.'

He bounded to his feet. 'Of course. I'll take you back to your car. You shall have all the time in the world to think about it. I shan't say a word to your brother until you tell me to. You shall be my guiding light.'

IO

It was clear from the moment that she and Mrs Jupp arrived in the morning that something terrible had happened to Mrs Weeks. So dramatic was her appearance that Edith and Alfred, who were sitting at breakfast, with one accord rose to their feet and helped her to a chair.

'What's happened? You don't look well. You shouldn't have come.'

Her face was greyish-white and swollen; she looked years older than she had a few days earlier. Without her make-up, hardly flattering in any real sense though that had been, her face betrayed a different personality, as if the garish colours had been a defiant mask concealing mere bewilderment. Her blonde hair was less carefully combed than usual, showing dark roots and what Edith for the first time suspected might be a toupee in the front.

'That boy,' she said in a voice trembling with emotion. 'It's that boy. I always said he'd come to no good. I've never had any trouble like that, none of my family have, we were always respectable people, we never mixed with those as weren't, gypsies and such. He might as well be a gypsy, that's what he is, no better than a gypsy, mixing with those travellers, so-called. "Travel, then," is what I said to them. "Call yourselves travellers — well, then, travel." Thieving vagabonds, more like. What he wants to get mixed up with that lot for beats me. It's his father come out in him, it's not from our side, we never had anything like that in our family.'

Edith pressed a mug of coffee into her hands and asked Mrs Jupp what had happened. Mrs Jupp, paler than usual but no more than usually subdued, replied that her son Sean had been arrested on suspicion of stealing car radios.

'There's a gang of them, they come from the travellers' camp. They've been doing it for some time, the police said, and television sets and videos too. I knew Sean was seeing them. He's had to go to the police station to give a statement.'

'We know what that means, don't we?' burst out Mrs Weeks. 'Being beaten up, that's what. They'll beat him up, that's what the police do nowadays. Do him good, I say. If he'd had a father to give him a good hiding.'

Mrs Jupp gave a small moan, possibly remembering good hidings she had had herself at the hands of her former husband. Alfred, unexpectedly firm, suggested that she should go to the police station to wait until Sean was allowed to leave, and then come back to fetch her mother. 'I'll run her home if you're not here by the end of the morning. Don't worry, it's a first offence and he was probably younger than the others, it won't be too bad.'

Mrs Jupp seemed to suggest in an increasingly incoherent manner that it might in fact not be a first offence. Alfred, thinking it best not to go into that possibility, ushered her towards the car.

Mrs Weeks, sidelined, watched her daughter leave. 'Being as you've got experience with the police,' she said to Alfred, following him to the door, 'you'd know what to do, of course.'

Ignoring this remark, Alfred said, 'He needs a job. I wonder if he's anything of a mechanic. John Jarrett needs someone he told me.'

'That John Jarrett,' began Mrs Weeks. But Alfred had gone, whistling to the dogs.

'What your poor mother would have said,' said Mrs Weeks.

'He'll learn,' said Edith. 'He's got you and his mother. You'll stand by him.' She followed Alfred out of the room before Mrs Weeks could express her determination to do nothing of the kind.

Alfred had disappeared. Edith put on her boots and coat and went out, thinking she might catch him up if he had gone for a walk. Outside she stood still, listening. It was very quiet. The sun had cleared the fog but the frost had not relaxed its grip; even the slightest branches of the trees were outlined in white. There was no wind; only stillness, sunlight, a white world with deep blue shadows and strong black-green tree trunks. The tall chestnut tree's leafless white branches claimed its own island of ground, an island on which she used to lie in summer in her pram looking up into the summer leaves. What would her mother have said, had asked Mrs Weeks, true to form. Edith did not know. The shape of the tree was deeply familiar, charged with private significances. Walking slowly over to stand beneath it, Edith remembered Derek in the days when they had been there together, but the idea of him seemed to slip easily into the idea of her father, his vehemence, his music, his struggle to catch harmonies he perhaps only half heard. And then under the tree it was her mother who came into her mind, whose quietness seemed always to restrain some kind of disapproval of her daughter's boldness — or was that no more than an old suspicion of Edith's own, perhaps unfounded? Quiet mornings. Edith thought, I don't have many quiet mornings. I prefer to be doing things, hurrying about, organizing people, talking, making things happen, even quite small things, I don't really like quiet mornings. Here, though, it is beautiful. Also clear. One should be able to think as clearly as this air is clear. And under this tree in clear but summer air, smelling of warm grass, of clean soft blankets, I bounced in a pram, but without knowing I bounced because I did not know the difference between myself and the outside world, between bouncing and being bounced, because frontiers which marked where one thing ended and another began were vague, and my senses, though humming, were inexperienced. In this undifferentiated world, as I moved and something restrained me (straps, a kind of harness), and as in the gently flickering light and shade under the tree I saw the green grass increase in area through the silver bars which supported the handle of the pram, all this was a sea of pleasurable sensation, marked in my memory only because of the surprise which then occurred, the running figure with arms outstretched, the expression of intense concern on the face, the jerk as the tipping pram was righted, the being snatched up and held against soft silk, kissed, consoled – but for what?

Surprise had lodged in the memory more deeply than other early experiences, causing it to surface years later under the same tree, an infant's surprise at an adult's offer of unnecessary consolation. Why should I have expected comfort, Edith thought, when all I was aware of was the crystal clarity of perfect bliss? My anxious mother, coming from the house to fetch me after my morning rest, saw that I was in danger of upsetting my pram; an incident from a quiet morning nearly sixty years ago. Was I even then very slightly despising her (although I cannot have known what scorn was)? And somewhere, because it is in my memory, I possess that bliss. It is part of my physical being, coming with me through all my lifetime. It is me, Edith thought, it is what I am.

Alfred had set off at speed to take the dogs up the valley, round the small beech wood and down again. 'I'm just going up and round,' his father used to say, leaving the house with Pibroch the snappy cairn. The walk took half an hour if you moved fast, three-quarters if you dawdled. Edith had been afraid that Alfred might have been annoyed by Mrs Weeks's remark about his familiarity with police procedures, but Alfred had long ceased to take offence at anything Mrs Weeks said, or to be surprised at how often it was at variance with what she actually did. It was true that he had once been very closely questioned by the police, though he had not been aware of his own danger until it had almost passed. It had not been fear which had threatened to consume him, so much as grief and guilt, on account of Lydia.

He strode up the hill, slipping from time to time on a frozen tussock and feeling the cold from the ice-bound earth on his face at the same time as he was aware of a faint contrary warmth on the back of his head from the sun. 'Adelaïde', he sang, breathlessly because he was walking, and slightly out of tune because he had never had a good ear (for which he believed his father had never forgiven him). 'Adelaïde', Beethoven's song, which he used to play on the gramophone over and over again in a crackling version sung by Jussi Björling which had belonged to his father. He had never learnt the whole song, nor did he understand the German in which it was sung, but he could do the oft-repeated 'Adelaïde' with feeling and also a line which he took to be a reference to a flower growing from the ashes of his heart, which had seemed not inappropriate at the time when he used to listen to the song often, trying to turn his grief into a quieter melancholy. He had wept for Lydia, sometimes with his arms round the slim black form of her whippet Nijinsky, who in a good mood would turn and turn in ever tightening circles but who would sit rocklike with lowered ears as if ashamed while Alfred wept; sometimes he would turn his sharp cold nose and breathe against Alfred's eyelids.

He thought about Lydia's past life but never understood it. It had sometimes seemed to be one thing, sometimes another. There was the Little Nell version, in which she and her dear old father kept the frame shop together, and distinguished artists sent her out for sandwiches while they discussed the world in general with her father until the day when the suave and worldly-wise Babbington offered her an expensive education and her father with tears in his eyes sacrificed his happiness so that she might better herself. There was another story, which surfaced whenever Alfred tentatively suggested that they should find out where her father had moved to when he left the frame shop, an unhappy story about a selfish drunk bringing women to the house who tried to shut Lydia out in the street, and about Babbington the kind rescuer, who had never seduced her and only wanted to make her into a perfect work of art. She said her mother was an artists' model who had died of tuberculosis, but she did not know her name. Questioned on any of these points, she would fly into a rage. 'Leave me alone. Why do you want to know? You're trying to catch me out. What does it matter, anyway?' Then he would quote extravagantly from Francis Thompson. 'What needest with thy tribe's black tents, / Who hast the red pavilion of my heart?' Mollified, she would giggle, and consent to step out again, face the world, accept its homage, elude its grasp.

'Sometimes I think you only want me as your walker,' he said, 'because you think we make a pretty pair.'

'So we do. How do I know why I love you?'

She loved him. What more did he want? That she should promise to love him for ever? He put to her the beauty of constancy, the romance of eternal fidelity. It failed to appeal; live for the moment, she said. There was also Babbington; there was no doubt she was still to some extent in thrall to him. She would occasionally have lunch with him at the Ritz; it was where he used to take her at half-term from school. Usually she returned in good spirits from these forays, with tales of skulduggery in the art world which she found highly amusing, but once she cried and said, 'He'll never let me go, don't let him take me back, I'm so afraid of him,' and Alfred, though he did not understand her, swore to save her. When she was calmer, he suggested that she should discontinue her meetings with Babbington, but by then her mood had changed and she said, 'How can I? He's my best friend.'

In the high days of their first year together none of this mattered; despite their cultivation of an appearance of beautiful idleness, in fact success, parties and love kept them intensely busy, and when they were not busy they were often tired, and so they slept. Lydia had a great capacity for sleep. In the intervals between modelling assignments — intervals she was now sufficiently in demand to insist on extending — she sometimes slept until evening. Alfred would come back from a day spent with Augustine on Emporium affairs to find her still in bed. She would have a bath and dress and they would go out. There was always a party, sometimes several; they would appear in some crowded room, accept a drink, look round and leave, until they ended up somewhere where Lydia liked the music, and then they would dance. Lydia had a way of holding her head high like a flamenco dancer; however vigorous or amusing the steps she chose to perform, she never lost this proud carriage, incongruous but graceful among a crowd of rock and roll dancers. Sometimes, tired of London life, they would stay with Alfred's parents for a few days, to the delight of his mother, who was already frail, and rather to the embarrassment of his father, who could not decide how to take Lydia and veered between heavy gallantry and a silence which was so unusual that Alfred knew it must be disapproving. He did not care. His relations with his father had never been as close as Edith's were. What was more, Lydia and their mutual enchantment took up all his emotional energy. He seemed to be inured not just to his father's disapproval but to his mother's pain. His mother was delighted by Lydia; that was what mattered. That she was dying was for another day.

'What you don't realize,' Augustine told him, 'is that fundamentally Lydia is bad news. She'll consume you. The awful void at the centre of her will suck you in like a whirlpool.'

Alfred never listened to Augustine in matters of the heart; he did not think him qualified to judge. Augustine remained on the friendliest of terms with Lydia, and took them both to America for the opening of the New York branch of Alfred's Clothes. Edwina came too. She and Augustine had married despite her father's opposition, which had anyway declined in proportion to Augustine's commercial success. Edwina had been cured of her alcoholism; this had not solved all their problems because she had fallen in love with a fellow addict whom she had met on the cure, but for the time being she and Augustine seemed on reasonably amicable terms and the

American trip was the happiest time the four of them spent together. The textile magnate who was backing their endeavours, and who was delighted by their spectacular success in New York, carried them off for a week to his ranch in Arizona and took them out to camp in hilarious luxury in the desert. They came home to find that Alfred's mother had died, sooner than expected although her cancer had been diagnosed some time previously. Edith had not been able to reach him with the news; she was looking after everything.

Hurrying to Somerset, Alfred found his father plunged into despair, which he tried to assuage by work. He had been working for some time on an orchestral suite about the death of King Arthur. He had nearly finished the first movement, which was perhaps enough in itself – in its final form it became, of all his music, the only piece which never lost its place on concert programmes – but he was not happy with it and wrestled with it obsessively after Janet's death. At first he had been overcome by grief, unable to control his sobs as he dwelt on her virtues and the unique nature of their marriage. Alfred found this embarrassing and was unable to respond as he felt he should; he also suffered from a conviction he could not possibly express that he had known his mother as no one else had and that he was the only person to mourn her true self. Edith, despite a similar shrinking from what she could not help seeing as a degree of self-indulgence on her father's part, was better able to sympathize with it. Both were relieved when he took up the King Arthur piece again, but his view of the world had darkened and he seemed to see the work as a threnody.

'This country is finished, we're in terminal decline, it's just a question of holding the situation until people accept the reality of it. Wilson and Heath, it makes no difference which, all they can do is manage the decline, and mouth meaningless words like "Commonwealth", and "special relationship with America". It's all nonsense. America thinks nothing of this country, they think we're sinking giggling into the sea.

Wasn't that what *Time* magazine said? The Commonwealth just means we're flooded with immigrants we can't afford to feed or house and haven't any work for, we're excluded from Europe by an alliance between France and Germany which we spent the last hundred years trying to prevent. And all we can do is indulge in the petty recriminations of a crumbling system. The unions want to wreck the economy – they don't care – they're expecting the victory of international communism. It'll come too very likely, after one government or another has to use force to control riots. We'll have a police state and the economy of an Eastern European country. That or anarchy. Either way it's barbarism. Arthur was fighting barbarism and he failed. He was the inheritor of Roman civilization. He tried to maintain it against the barbarians, but it had lost the will to excel and he lost, he went down. As we shall do. We've lost the will to excel.'

'Perhaps we've lost the capacity to change,' said Edith. 'And we'll get it back, and reform and adjust and be all right. What about that?'

'Oh, you can reform your dustbin men. Or your kindergartens. But you've forgotten what it's like to live in a country that has self-respect. You were a child when we last were a great nation.'

'Being a minor nation might have compensations,' said Alfred. 'We could stop thinking of ourselves as belonging to any particular nation and become citizens of the world. We could respect the world rather than ourselves.'

'Rubbish. You've been listening to some airy-fairy hippy nonsense.'

They could not comfort him because he did not want to be comforted, and he could not compose because he could not find a musical language to express an anger and a disappointment he had never wanted to express before. His anger was against England. He had been proud of having worked his way up from humble beginnings. His marriage, his highly creditable reputation as a composer, albeit not of the very highest rank, the money he had been able to earn, the education he had been able to give his children, his position in a social hierarchy he revered, all now seemed hollow; England had let him down. God had let him down too, by taking away his wife; but God and England had always been inextricably entwined in his scheme of things, and it was perhaps better to let England take the brunt of his disillusion. He used to urge his children to rejoice, now it seemed he resented their reluctance to rage.

Alfred was not hurt by his father's curtness. He was used to it. As a child he had not been able to sing in tune; he felt it all stemmed from that. And then he had no proper profession, had chucked up a good job in the City to make cakes and design clothes, activities his father considered effeminate. The fact that he appeared to have a beautiful mistress and even to make money only proved his effrontery. He was riding for a fall. Which was true, though not precisely in the way his father envisaged.

Alfred went back to London as soon as he felt he could. Lydia needed him. She had a new friend called Hughie, a very small, very young man with a bad complexion and a charming smile; he entertained her with his chatter, which was a mixture of snobbish gossip and theories of the universe. The two were often combined. No theory about cosmic rays or interventions from outer space but was enhanced in his eyes by the fashionable status or ancient lineage of whoever had first made it known to him; he laughed at this weakness in himself but made no effort to resist it. He had become Lydia's constant companion during the time in which Alfred had been preoccupied with family affairs; Lydia did not like to be alone. Alfred found him amusing enough, and helpful domestically; he was forever making cups of tea. He had plentiful supplies of marijuana, but preferred LSD; it was the consciousness-expanding drug of the future, he said, quoting Timothy Leary and Aldous Huxley. One evening Alfred and Lydia had a bad trip and found themselves alone in the bedroom of their little house, terrified and paranoiac. Alfred had to hold on to Lydia to prevent her climbing out on to the roof because she said someone was coming up the stairs, though the door was locked. She broke away from him and ran to the telephone; he heard her gasping for help and repeating that there was a key under the flower-pot. Babbington arrived in their bedroom, immaculately dark-suited and unsmiling. Lydia rushed into his arms; they left Alfred crouched in a corner of the room, trembling and sweating.

He did not leave the house for three days. He had recovered his nerve, but he was afraid that if Lydia came back and he was not there she might disappear for ever. On the fourth morning she came; there were explanations, tears, an apparent return to normal.

Looking back, Alfred thought – walking now on the icy hillside – that in fact something had changed at that time; Lydia had seen something which had badly frightened her, perhaps just in the inevitability of her own flight to Babbington. Unusually for these quiet, frost-bound days a sharp wind had come up; it made Alfred's face ache as he walked back down the hill. The dogs had disappeared into the wood behind him. As he approached the house, he saw Edith standing in the farmyard beyond the chestnut tree, her back towards him, looking at the buildings. He felt a quick annoyance. She was always wanting to stir things up. He needed to be left alone. He was busy, she interrupted his work. Her presence turned his thoughts towards parts of his life he usually left well alone. But as he came closer, he saw how the cold wind blew her hair away from her face, exposing its vulnerability; she was getting old, had wanted to achieve things, was worried about her daughter.

When she saw him she said, 'I was remembering how it looked in the summer, with those carts and the horses and the fire in the middle.'

'I always thought you disapproved of all that.'

'I expect I felt left out.'

But he was right; she had disapproved. She had been afraid that Alfred might become addicted to drugs, not realizing that he was too much of a hypochondriac to become addicted to anything. She was also affronted by the high status accorded by Hughie and his friends to the irrational. She believed passionately that there was nothing which should not be submitted to the light of reason; it distressed her to see it mocked. The merry whimsicality with which Hughie, footloose in the world of ideas, skipped from one notion to another, plucking what he pleased to make a posy of fancies with which to brighten a world made new, maddened her by its incoherence and irritated her by making her feel a prig. Alfred had urged her to treat the house exactly as she had done in their father's lifetime, but her visits became increasingly infrequent; she was busy in London, what with Sarah now at day school, and her council work and her schools committees, and the part-time work she did to make ends meet now that she was divorced (this was before the advent of Derek). It was easier to stay away, to leave the field to Lydia, who hardly seemed to notice when Hughie told her that love was where it was at. When he said it to Edith, she felt her face set like a fallen soufflé.

'You go on with your work,' she said now. 'I'll take Mrs Weeks home if Mrs Jupp doesn't reappear.'

'Poor Mrs Weeks, she has to be endured.'

'I wish she could be persuaded to retire.'

'No such luck. I've tried. She's simply one of my burdens. I haven't many.'

Something had gone wrong with Beryl's filing. The landscape of the Mendips seemed to have been unaccountably extended, the expanses of daisy-strewn grass, white sheep and low grey walls giving way to bare heights, rock-strewn valleys devoid of trees or water, the stark contrast of a ravaged land under an ancient sun. This was Sicily. Muttering irritably, Alfred searched for the correct file. This was Sicily with Raffaella, who had raged to him about politics while he recorded the enormous landscapes for which the magazine had asked.

Raffaella was a communist and a polemical journalist; he had worked with her on several articles about the south of Italy. Sicily had been at the time the strong medicine he needed; his sorrows were briefly subsumed in the ancient and apparently irredeemable griefs of that ravaged and enrapturing island. He discovered its grand, denuded landscape and the astonishing beauty of its neglected buildings, while Raffaella inveighed against the poverty and corruption; she claimed that the Mafia would never take a woman seriously and that as a result she could write with impunity about political scandals, mysterious disappearances of government grants and the destruction being wrought by the oil industry. Her fiery articles attracted attention but had no influence on events; after a time she went into television in Rome and became part of a life Alfred did not find congenial. He lost touch with her but retained an affectionate memory of her courage and intelligence if not of her extraordinarily piercing voice. It was she who, when he had told her a little about Lydia, said, 'You have to go back. You have to forgive yourself.' In the end he thought he would try.

Sicily had seemed the fiery crater in which the whole of Mediterranean civilization flashed and gleamed and reddened the sky; Pembrokeshire was a remote outpost of that same world, sobered by the Atlantic wind, softened by sweet rains, its cliffs in the spring adorned less abundantly by the same wild flowers. It was spring when Alfred first went there, with Lydia; autumn when he returned.

That spring Lydia had been restless, or perhaps she had been ill. It had not been a good winter. She had more or less given up modelling and when the weather drove most of the hippies back to Notting Hill Gate she was bored. Hughie was still there but his faith in LSD had wavered and he had turned to politics; he went several times to London to join demonstrations against the war in Vietnam outside the

American Embassy and returned obsessed by police persecution and convinced he was being watched. There was a red-haired girl called Marilyn who had been left behind by someone and who seemed to be in love with Lydia; Lydia exploited her devotion mercilessly but in the end let her see that she was bored by her. Alfred and Lydia went to London to get away from Hughie and Marilyn. Lydia was persuaded by her agent to go to Milan for a fashion show; Alfred meanwhile worked out an agreement with Augustine by which Augustine bought most of Alfred's shares in the business and Alfred was paid a small salary as a consultant. Augustine, on the way to his first fortune, was nevertheless reluctant.

'I feel I'm dropping the pilot,' he said. 'I'll have no one to talk to. What if I lose my soul?'

'You haven't got one,' said Alfred rudely. 'And besides you can always ring me up.'

He could think of nothing but living with Lydia in Somerset. He never believed, afterwards, that because it had not turned out that way it could never have happened. He had the house, and the money from Augustine; Lydia had the Swiss bank account which Babbington had arranged for her when her earnings began to soar. He could go on with his photography; Lydia could either do nothing, or if she was bored she could go in for horse-dealing with John Jarrett with whom she had struck up an unlikely friendship; they had gone together last summer to Priddy Fair where Lydia had bought a stout young cob whom she rode as recklessly as the horse, a cautious animal, would allow.

Augustine was not optimistic. 'Lydia needs the bright lights,' he said. 'You don't understand that girl. She needs what she's used to. She can't believe she exists unless she sees her face in a glossy magazine every week.'

Afterwards Alfred thought it was probably Babbington Lydia needed in order to believe in her own existence, not photographs of herself, nor drugs. Babbington was her careless creator and her casual destroyer. Alfred came to be tormented by the thought that he had been wrong to take her beyond Babbington's reach, but at the time he said to Augustine, 'That's all changed. You'll see.'

Indeed when Lydia came back from Milan, it seemed she could not wait to leave London. They found Hughie and Marilyn sunk in gloom; they had been unable to work the central heating and had run out of food. Lydia lost her temper and told them both to leave. Alfred drove them to the station.

'She's become so hard,' Hughie said. 'I never would have believed it. It must be the country air. She's a termagant, a virago.' He climbed out of the car and searched in the pockets of his outsized overcoat. 'Here.' He fished out a plastic bag of hash. 'Coals of fire. Give it to her with my love.' He wandered away towards the London train, followed by the tear-stained Marilyn, who was carrying his Afghan carpet-bag as well as her own.

When Alfred gave Lydia the hash, she swore and ran upstairs; he heard her furiously opening drawers and deduced that she must have had some other drugs which Hughie had taken. She said nothing when she came downstairs and nor did Alfred. She knew he did not think drugs were good for her and he saw no point in nagging, but he was distressed by her jumpiness during the next few days, believing it to show that she had been taking more than he had suspected. She accused him of failing to understand her. 'I am a damaged personality,' she said. Was he not interested? He said he was interested but in this instance did not agree with her. She said he was an old Nanny thinking everything could be cured by fresh air and exercise. 'And regular meals,' he said. So he didn't think she cooked enough, so he wanted a little woman to cook and have babies, and anyway why did he put up with her when she was so nasty to him?

'Because I think I can do it,' he said grimly.

'Do what? You think you can do what?'

122

'I'm not going to tell you. I'll tell you when I've done it.'
But he meant, save her. He thought he could save her.

He suggested that they should go away for a week. Lawrence Raven had told them about his childhood holidays in Wales with his grandparents; why not spend a few days in Pembrokeshire? She said her whippet would fall off the cliffs. Alfred arranged to leave him with John Jarrett. Initially reluctant, Lydia came wonderfully to life when they reached St David's. She walked for miles in the sun and wind and sometimes soft rain; the cliffs were covered with wild flowers. Lydia's anxieties seemed to dissolve, her funniness and charm to return. They sat on springy grass high above the sea, sheltered by scrubby bushes on which a stonechat perched decoratively against the sky; Alfred began to unpack their lunch. Lydia said quite solemnly, 'I am perfectly and completely happy.'

As far as Alfred could remember, he simply replied cheerfully, 'So am I.' Should he have given some other answer, been more emotional, attempted some profundity? He was opening a bottle of wine. She wandered away. He cut some bread, began to butter it. Did he hear something? A wingbeat, perhaps, a flag unfurled. He lay back in the sun to await her return, shut his eyes, heard laboured breathing and sat up surprised. A youth, scarlet in the face and sweating.

'Down there. Just now. Someone fell off the cliff.'

Scrabbling with reckless speed down the rocks, the boy behind him. 'She jumped. I saw her jump.'

The torn, discarded image gathered into his arms and the strange high voice he did not recognize as his own. 'You shouldn't have done it. You shouldn't have done it. You shouldn't have done it.'

11

Edith, dropping Mrs Weeks at the door of her cottage, commented favourably on her neat front garden. Mrs Weeks said she supposed it would all go now, if Sean went to prison.

'He does it for you, then?'

'He's a good boy that way.' She had spent the whole of the journey saying what a bad boy he was and, seeming suddenly to realize this, she stopped halfway out of the car, fell back into her seat and began to fumble in her handbag.

'Don't worry,' said Edith.

Mrs Weeks found a handkerchief and blew her nose. Edith patted her on the knee.

'You're good people,' said Mrs Weeks. She got out of the car, more successfully this time, and turned before shutting the door to add, 'Not like your parents of course.'

'Of course not,' said Edith, relieved to see a return of Mrs Weeks's more usual manner. 'Of course we're not as good as our parents.'

Driving back to the house, it occurred to her that if Charles Warburton's scheme came to fruition there would be work for John Jarrett. Those off-road vehicles would certainly need a lot of repair and maintenance if they were going to be thrown around by drivers like Charles.

Alfred was talking on the telephone to Sarah.

'She's driving Mrs Weeks home. She said I was to tell you to pull yourself together.'

'Really? That's the sort of thing I usually say to you.'

'That's what I told her.'

'I can't make out why she's so upset. I'd have thought

she'd have been pleased that I'm not going to live on the other side of the world.'

'She thinks you're endangering your marriage.'

'That's what she said. Robert's pleased, anyway. He's always thought she didn't really like him.'

'Of course she likes him. She's always boasting about him.'

'Really? Oh, good. Well anyway, who's she to talk, with two divorces and more or less cohabiting with a seedy old hack? At her age.'

'Don't you like Hubert?'

'I adore him. It's he who says he's a seedy old hack, not me.'

'She says it's because she knows how horrible divorce is that she doesn't want you to do it.'

'Of course I'm not going to do it. Robert and I get on very well.'

'She's worried about propinquity.'

'What?'

'Dashing young account executives. Nubile secretaries.'

'How depressing.'

'Yes.'

'It's the golden cage, you see. We're in the golden cage. That's what it's called. You have to earn as much as you possibly can between the ages of twenty-five and forty because you can't get jobs after that and you've got to earn enough to educate your children and live on for the rest of your life. I've got to go, I'm taking fifteen children to the pantomime. Tell her I'll ring her this evening, or tomorrow. Probably tomorrow.'

'I'll tell her. I'll tell her about the golden cage too. How awful for you.'

'Don't sound so worried. We'll survive. Alexander, stop hitting Hereward. Oh, he's not called Hereward. Probably just as well. Herald? Oh, Harold. I must go, Elfred, the New Zealand nannies are champing at the bit.'

'Dear Jeannie,' wrote Edith. 'It's cold and I am feeling

125

haunted by the past. I don't like it because I have always been so keen to grab myself a future. Anyway I owe you a letter.'

Jeannie Mackintosh; her old supporter, had left London some time ago and moved to a small town in the west of Ireland, where she had started a craft shop. Her husband, Max, the unsuccessful architect, had died, and their five extraordinarily cheerful children had scattered around the world, earning their livings in a variety of mostly adventurous ways. Jeannie was as she had always been, only even larger. Edith had been to see her. She had flowed out from the back of the shop in an extravagance of hand-woven wraps and cries of joy. 'It's the good woman in politics herself, I can't believe it.' The voice, rather breathless and sounding always as if it had had to fight its way out through suppressed laughter, was a little deeper, to match the increased stoutness; it used to be high and girlish. Not everyone had liked her. Lal used to say, 'Here comes the earth mother, umbrellas up,' which was mean, because though she did spit occasionally in the urgency of her desire to communicate there was no question of a shower. Edith had never thought that she was an earth mother, either. It was just that she saw everything in decisive terms of right and wrong, and, having five children and not much money, she saw it as her duty to devote herself not only to their well-being but to their education, supplementing in every way she could the rather meagre schooling they received at their local state school. She did her best to help Max in his career as well, frequently surprising and occasionally offending comparative strangers by telling them how much their houses were in need of improvement or extension or even abandonment in favour of something completely new and wonderful built by Max, who would often be standing near by looking desperately embarrassed. They went to Ireland eventually because Max was going to build some houses for a holiday enterprise of some sort, but he died and the children grew up, and there Jeannie was with her craft shop, the mainstay, as it quickly appeared to Edith, of a whole little township of lame ducks. It was Jeannie who was the good woman, of course. She was the only one among all the committee workers who never seemed to want anything for herself. All the others at some time or other wanted either Edith's job, or in the case of Betty Mainwaring her husband, or more of her gratitude than anyone else was getting, or a position of power or prestige or public importance, or their name in the paper or a job for their son or a place for their daughter at the better of the local schools. Only Jeannie turned up regularly to put leaflets in envelopes or to walk the streets delivering them or to march with her children to demand state nursery schools or simply to soothe people by her apparently limitless admiration for everything they did. Except Lal. Jeannie never cared for Lal. When he talked about politics in his flippant Oxford way, she would say, 'That's wicked. You can't mean it,' and ignore him. He said she was absurdly naïve, which she was. Edith found her very encouraging.

Jeannie complained of Lal's cynicism. He taught post-colonial cultural studies at the polytechnic, and made jokes about the jargon of the subject, claiming that he devoted his whole course to Third World Cinema and that since there was no Third World Cinema his students spent their time studying pre-war American B-movies, ostensibly for purposes of comparison; according to him, his courses were over-subscribed and everyone was happy. He came to one of Edith's meetings because it was held in the building where he worked, and stayed to talk. He seemed to think helping her campaign was as much of a joke as everything else, but he provided her with some good slogans. In fact it was he who suggested that people would take her more seriously if she stood not as an Independent but as a representative of the Independent Citizens Party, even though no such party at that time existed. The party's manifesto was worked out one morning over a cup of coffee, and printed on the technical college's equipment after hours; it attracted a wholly unexpected amount of attention, people appeared from nowhere wanting to form branches in various other parts of the country, and by the time Derek came on the scene with his confident talk about marketing techniques there was something ready to be marketed. Derek's ability to call on a variety of more or less famous people, most of them not previously connected with politics, to come and speak on Edith's behalf, raised the profile of the new party in a way which was extremely heartening to its first supporters, who for all their enthusiasm had had until then quite modest expectations. Derek's other success had been in promoting Edith as a speaker on general subjects, particularly in discussion programmes, such as *Any Questions?* on the radio. She was fearless and funny, and soon became a regular member of the panel. Lal was particularly good at guessing what subjects were likely to come up, so making sure that she was well briefed. All through that first election Lal remained light-hearted. By the time the next election came round he had become her enemy.

'There is an unbridgeable chasm between us,' he said, wrinkling his delicate features fastidiously. 'It is merely stupid of you not to recognize it.'

'I recognize that for some reason you have decided to consider yourself a black activist. I don't quite know what it means, but there it is.'

'It means that if necessary I would kill you.'

'That's absurd. Anyway I won't kill you, however idiotic you are.'

He jumped to his feet, trembling. 'That means that we shall win.'

'It doesn't. It means that you or your children will sooner or later come round to my way of thinking because it is a better way of thinking. I wish you would go away, Lal. I feel very tired and disheartened.'

'How tired and disheartened do you think I am?' He burst into tears. 'I am battered, battered to pieces by your colonialism and your horrible, horrible kindness.'

He rushed from the room and down the stairs. She saw him running down the street, light-footed and fast as ever. She thought he would soon come back, but he never did.

'It is extraordinary,' Edith wrote to Jeannie, sitting by the fire after having driven Mrs Weeks home,

how whole pockets of feeling can be stored away, forgotten for years, and then quite unexpectedly emerge in all their pristine fervour, time having wrought no modification at all. This morning I remembered exactly – but so exactly it seemed much more than a memory – falling out of my pram under the big tree beside this house. And then flashes of scenes with my parents or with Alfred keep coming back to me. And I've been thinking of Derek because there's a man who's come to live nearby who wears the same sort of jersey. And now, because I'm writing to you and remembering our old campaigning days, I'm suddenly furious with Lal. What a silly man he was. I thought he was my friend. I suppose I was proud to have a black friend. He should have warned me things were going wrong. There I was banging on about how wrong it was to have separate nursery schools for immigrant children because we wanted them all to be part of our own culture, and suddenly there were all those completely unknown people yelling at me about black power, and then the even more horrible shaven-headed yobbos making monkey noises and scratching their armpits. Why didn't Lal warn me? He must have seen it coming. Perhaps he didn't. He never spoke to all those Jamaicans and Nigerians who lived around there, he was much too upper-class and Oxford-educated. I suppose it was guilt that made him ditch me – he was as much a symbol of hated privilege as I was. Do you remember when I was mocked for having a middle-class accent – which would have horrified my mother who thought middle-class was synonymous with common – and I lost my head and said my grandfather was a shoemaker and they howled me down and I was so ashamed to have let myself be provoked into replying at all? But what would my father have thought of my being discriminated against for coming from the wrong class, he to whom having attained affiliation to the upper classes meant so much?

They were right, I suppose, looking back. It's the hardest thing of all for someone like me to have to recognize that someone else will do what I want to do better than I can. I was not the right person for the times. When I first went into the House, I never dreamt that the pretty woman who came quickly up to me like a busy hen and congratulated me with such sweetness and such clear blue eyes and bustled off again was the woman whose hour was about to strike. She didn't look like the Angel of Destiny. She looked a bit common actually. There's a lot of luck in these things. I know you boil and bubble at the very name of Thatcher, but she did what everyone else wanted to do and what Wilson and Heath and Barbara Castle had all tried to do – pull things together, curb the unions, curb inflation. I know she went mad later, but can you wonder? No one should be allowed that amount of power for more than a few years – it's like human blood to a tiger.

Don't think I'm making ridiculous comparisons. I never wanted to be more than a useful bottle-washer as you know. I'd have liked to go on though, if Derek hadn't put paid to all that.

Alfred pushed aside his prints of Sicily and went back to the Mendips. He looked for caves and underground rivers, remembering how he had been with his mother to such places and how when she read him George Macdonald's stories he had known that the goblins' mines were somewhere very near,

just underneath the hill; but he could not find any photographs and wondered whether the clear pictures he had were
only in his head. His thoughts returned to his recent telephone
conversation with Sarah. Perhaps he had become selfish,
living alone, protecting himself from anxiety. Perhaps he
ought to have been more concerned about Sarah, of whom
he was fond and who seemed to have money worries. Should
he give her some money? But he had very little left, apart
from his earnings; his chief asset was the house. If he died, she
could have the house, perhaps to sell. But he had no inclina-
tion to die, none at all. It was Edith, of course, who had
shaken him out of his peaceful isolation; Sarah as usual had
sounded perfectly cheerful. Perhaps Edith was wrong.

Abandoning his search, he went downstairs and found
Edith sitting in front of the fire.

'Perhaps you're wrong,' he said.

'What about?' she asked mildly, putting aside her letter.

'Sarah. Maybe she knows what's best for her. She always
seems so sure of things.'

'People who seem sure of things can be just as wrong as
people who are riddled with doubts. I know. I'm sure of
things. But it's often quite a provisional sureness. It's just that
I don't like indecision.'

'What does Hubert think?'

'Hubert?'

'About Sarah.'

'He doesn't know. About her going to Hong Kong, I
mean. It hadn't come up when I left London.'

Alfred wondered why Edith, who usually picked up the
telephone at the slightest provocation, had not spoken to
Hubert about something which was so important to her.

Edith, trying to forestall that thought, said, 'I was just
going to ring up Rose Brown.'

'Is she a friend of Sarah's?'

'Not exactly, but she knows all about her, and she's such a
nice person.'

'She wrote quite a bad book about Madame de Sévigné.'

'You can't have read it. You're not at all interested in Madame de Sévigné.'

'No, but our mother used to have her letters by her bed, so I had a look at it in a bookshop. I didn't think much of it.'

'How could you tell if you only looked at it in a bookshop? Besides, you can be a nice person without writing a good book about Madame de Sévigné. How very irritating you are, Alfred.'

'You have told me three times since you have been here what a nice person Rose Brown is.'

'Have I? Well she is a nice person. But I won't tell you again.'

'All right. Then I won't ask you why you haven't rung up Hubert.'

Edith put on her glasses, picked up her pen and her unfinished letter, and said distantly, 'I don't see any particular reason to ring up Hubert.'

'Apart from anything else, he's known Sarah for years, they've always got on extremely well.'

'Then she can ring him up herself.'

'I think Sarah would like it if you and Hubert got married,' said Alfred.

Edith was briefly silent, shocked by his raising a subject on which he already knew her views.

'Two marriages are quite enough,' she said eventually. 'Besides, we're too old. It would be ridiculous. People marry to have children.'

'Companionship in old age?'

'We have that already. It's a perfectly convenient arrangement, in which we keep our independence. I couldn't bear to live with Hubert all the time. He smokes too much.'

'Couldn't you ask him to give it up?'

'Of course not.'

'But why?'

'Because if I asked him and he did, then I'd have to marry

him, wouldn't I?' she said irritably. 'Do stop going on about it.'

'All right. I'll go and find John Jarrett. If we're going to suggest he gives Sean Jupp a job we'd better get on with it.'

He called his white lurcher, shut the other two dogs into the room with Edith and set off towards the village. He walked fast, the lurcher shadowing him. The road had been salted and he walked in the middle of it rather than on the icy pavement. The silence of the great cold still held his surroundings enthralled. There was no sound of traffic, or of wind in the frozen trees, or birds. A dog barked some way away, giving rise to a slight responsive growl from Jinks, whose softly scuffling pads on the gritty road surface were otherwise the only sound apart from his own footsteps.

Edith had not liked his mentioning Hubert. They seldom discussed their emotional lives – they never had – while knowing at the same time that the other was well enough informed. There were certain delicacies in their relationship, from which they did not, generally speaking, diverge. Displays of emotion were as unthinkable as angry confrontations. After Lydia's death Alfred had felt the strength of Edith's support, but he could not remember that she had actually said anything at all. She had hugged him briefly outside the courtroom where the inquest was held, that was all. Even that was almost too much, but she had turned away quickly and said something to Augustine, who had come down with her from London. Alfred had telephoned Augustine to tell him what had happened. Augustine had got in touch with Edith and the two of them had set off for Wales. To Alfred's distress Babbington had also appeared at the inquest, having been contacted by the police who had discovered that he had been Lydia's guardian. He had been remote and authoritative. There was nothing surprising about the sad story, he implied, the poor girl was quite unbalanced. She had been having treatment, he had begged her not to discontinue it.

The fact was that Lydia had given up her treatment soon

after she met Alfred. She said the psychiatrist kept trying to force his attentions on her and had threatened to hypnotize her if she did not submit. Alfred had been deeply shocked and thought the man ought to be reported to some authority or other, but later he thought perhaps Lydia had over-dramatized the story. He told it to the police; he told everything to the police, because they interviewed him for hours at a time and he could think of no particular reason not to answer their questions. At one stage he realized he was in danger of being accused of Lydia's murder and had just enough will to survive to feel relieved that there had been a witness, but when halfway through the interviews the tone of the inquiry changed and he realized that he was no longer suspected he felt a terrible depression, as if the danger had been the only thing sustaining him. At the inquest he had to say that before she walked away from him to the top of the cliff from which she threw herself, she had said that she was completely happy. The coroner asked him whether in his view she would have wanted to end her life at a point at which she was completely happy, and he had gripped the front of the witness box and answered fairly steadily, 'Yes.' A small collective sigh seemed to come from the few people sitting in the damp court-room. He felt that they understood, and was afraid he might break down, but he glanced quickly at Edith and saw her lips set in a tight line. She understood, all right; she was thinking that it was just the sort of idiotic thing Lydia would have done. No sentimentalist, Edith. It steadied his nerve.

Babbington had driven off in his Bentley, leaving Edith and Augustine to take the train with Alfred. Alfred remembered Babbington's slightly questioning look as he stood by the car before getting into it, as if he might have been thinking of entering into conversation; Alfred, on the other side of the road, had turned away. He had not seen Babbington since. He must remember to ask Edith if she thought he was dead. She would know; she read obituaries. Everyone seemed to have obituaries these days. If nothing else, Babbington's brief appearance in the witness box at the trial of Stephen Ward would have secured him a mention somewhere. Alfred slipped Jinks on to the lead to walk through the village, towards John Jarrett's new bungalow, which was the other side of the church. Alfred had not seen young Sean Jupp for some time and did not know whether he would be much use as a mechanic, but there seemed no harm in suggesting that John Jarrett might give him a trial.

Edith jumped up to answer the telephone, expecting Sarah; but it was Johnny, her first husband.

'Just confirming dinner tomorrow,' he said. 'You are coming, aren't you?'

'Did Alfred say we would?'

'Yes, he did. Do sound more enthusiastic. You'll enjoy it. It's absolutely our last farewell party. We've had two already. I've asked someone you haven't seen for years. It'll be a surprise.'

'I hate surprises. Do tell me who.'

'Certainly not.'

'If it's Charles Warburton, I've seen him already.'

'Good old Charlie. Did he try to sell you insurance? Not yet? He will, he will. We'll see you about eight, then. Warm clothes, heating's on the blink.'

How could Alfred have let her in for such a thing? Heating on the blink indeed. And who could be this person she hadn't seen for years? It must be someone she and Johnny used to see when they were married, one of his gambling friends perhaps; it was sure to be someone she had never cared for, Johnny had an infallible gift for getting that sort of thing wrong. Edith liked to think that she had reached a stage and condition of life which meant that she could choose her own company; earlier obligations, whether to a husband or a profession, had gone. If she had to have dealings with someone uncongenial, it was for purposes of her own, whether advantage, duty or kindness. Now the prospect of an evening which might well be long and would certainly be cold, spent in the company of people for whom she knew she would find it hard to conceal her lack of charitable feeling, seemed an infringement of her liberty. She went back to the fire, put on another log and sat down again, too much out of humour to go on with her letter to Jeannie.

The room was lined with bookshelves, mostly filled with books familiar to her from her parents' time; some had been added by Alfred, but he kept most of his own books in his bedroom. There were the faded pink volumes of the *Collected Works* of Robert Louis Stevenson which had been given to her mother as a wedding present, and the blue library edition of Byron which might have been a wedding present too, rows of Hardy, Kipling, Jane Austen, her father's favourite Somerset Maugham, Compton Mackenzie; then there were works of history, everything G. M. Trevelyan had written, Gibbon's *Decline and Fall of the Roman Empire* in the unabridged edition, some volumes of Lord Acton's *Essays*, biographies of composers and admirals, reminiscences of life in India. There was a shelf of Arthurian matter, Malory's *Morte d'Arthur*, Tennyson's *Idylls of the King*, novels by Meriol Trevor and Rosemary Sutcliffe, poetry by John Masefield. Her father must have read all that when he was working on his *King Arthur Suite*, which had occupied him intermittently for so many years. He had taken his own line about the story in the end, making his King Arthur the defender of a Christian civilization left vulnerable by the decadence of the Romans. Perhaps the idea had been behind the patriotic pageant Edith remembered so imperfectly from the war years, King Arthur and Winston Churchill improbably merged in her father's imagination. 'Sing then, brother, sing, giving everything.' But she had forgotten the words, and the emotion, which she did remember, had become embarrassing, like an early love affair in which one had made a fool of oneself. After that time the themes had continued to haunt him but had never come together to his satisfaction. Only a fragment remained, the piece still played more than any of his other works except one or two of the songs, the Andante for Horn and Strings, *In Arthur's Cave*. Edith found it intensely sad because she thought of it as an elegy for her mother; he had written most of it before her death, but in the knowledge of its imminence. After her death his grief had been so mixed with self-pity and even a kind of petulance, that Edith every time she heard the piece was afraid of finding it sentimental, as some of his songs were sentimental, and each time instead she was moved by its sombre sense of mystery. Arthur was in his cave, just there somewhere beneath the familiar hills, beside one of those silently slipping underground streams, the king who slept while the distant horns called on him to wake. The strings swept into discord, the king stirred, but the sounds of storm baffled the horns and he slept on, the call of his people dying on the wind. It did not matter to Edith that the king had probably never existed; it mattered that he had betrayed her father.

12

The young man who stood on the doorstep wore a black baseball cap with what seemed to Alfred an exaggeratedly large peak. Beneath it his face, pale, dumbly hostile and marked by blotches where spots had been scratched and then overlaid by whiteish ointment, was fringed by long straight hair of ferociously tangled aspect. He was dressed in clothes too small for him. His bony red wrists and large hands protruded from the sleeve of a tattered bomber jacket. He wore black trainers with silver stripes, from the holes in which sprouted large pieces of once-white sock. He appeared to have a bad cold.

'This is Sean,' said Mrs Jupp apologetically.

Alfred asked them both in, thankful for Edith's presence.

'He's come to thank you,' said Mrs Jupp determinedly, 'haven't you, Sean?'

Sean was overcome by a coughing fit. Mrs Jupp explained that John Jarrett had offered him two weeks' work on trial. Edith began to question him briskly about his forthcoming prosecution. He answered dolefully, admitting that he had a previous conditional discharge. Mrs Jupp sniffed dismally.

'It's those people he got in with, those travellers. Think nothing of breaking the law.'

'Of course they don't,' said Alfred. 'They're breaking it by staying where they're not legally allowed to, living in vehicles most of which are not licensed. They get into the habit of thinking nothing of the law. It's very unfortunate.'

'What did you do?' Edith asked Sean. 'I mean the first time.'

The boy, too big for the small kitchen chair on which he

was sitting, suddenly jerked into life; the chair over-balanced and he fell off.

'He's that clumsy,' said Mrs Jupp, blushing.

Sean picked himself up. He looked at his mother with an apologetic, slightly clownish smile.

'What did you do?' asked Edith again, righting the chair for him.

'Climbed a tree,' he said, seemingly unable to stop smiling.

'I didn't know that was illegal.'

''Tis when they want to cut it down.'

'Ah. Where was this?'

'Over Hampshire way. They were building a road.'

'So I suppose you tied yourself to the tree, once you'd climbed it?'

He put out both huge hands sideways and shrugged, raising his eyebrows comically. 'What else could I do?'

'Saving the countryside?'

'We'll have none left, will we?' he said with sudden animation. 'They'll have it all motorway soon, all the way from Athens to Cork, that's what I've heard. It's our land, isn't it?'

'It belongs to the various different people who own it, really,' said Alfred mildly. 'The rest of us have access to it as long as we don't do any damage to it.'

'No, but Alfred,' said Edith, 'it's much better for Sean to be tying himself to trees than stealing car radios.'

'I shouldn't have thought one necessarily precluded the other.'

'Have you stopped stealing car radios, Sean?' asked Edith.

'Yea, they're stupid, those people. They go on to cars, joy-riding and that. I'm not into that.'

'Don't you either I should think not,' interposed Mrs Jupp in one furious breath.

'Are you in a different group then now? Have you got leaders?'

'It's all committees like, we don't have leaders. We just do what we're told by the committee. We're all in the committee, I think.'

'Is there someone you follow then yourself? Someone you admire?'

He nodded enthusiastically. 'I follow Percival,' he said.

'Is that his real name?' asked Edith, surprised.

'I don't know. I never heard any other. I think he's American or something. Or Dutch. Dutch, I think. He looks like Boris Becker.'

'What does he know about the English countryside?' said Alfred scornfully.

'A lot,' said Sean earnestly. 'He knows it all. And all these plans and everything, from the European Commission, and all the laws about it. He goes to all these meetings.'

'And lives in a broken-down bus in a lay-by?' said Alfred.

'He's got a bender, it's nice, him and Trish.'

'Well now, listen, Sean,' said Edith. 'I know a lot about laws, too, because I used to be a magistrate, and I can tell you it's a very bad idea to get a police record. If you go on demonstrations, just don't be the one that gets hauled up in court, it's not worth it. And don't get dared to do things by the others. Are they older than you? I expect they dared you to steal from cars, didn't they? You have to grow out of that, it's just silly. And if you're interested in what's happening about roads, you should learn about it properly. Which bit of countryside is being destroyed? Does it matter? What wildlife is there? What do the local people want? Get the facts. Listen to Boris Becker and ask him questions. And don't ever not turn up for work on one of the days John Jarrett is expecting you.'

'OK,' said Sean cheerfully.

He drove off with a good deal of unnecessary revving up of the engine, his mother expostulating beside him.

Alfred said to Edith, 'Wasn't that rather irresponsible?'

'What, me?'

'Of course you. You're encouraging him to go on mixing with those frightful travellers. You don't know anything about them. It's people like you who protect them. Country people know what they're like. They loathe them. They're filthy and disgusting, they crap on people's doorsteps, they take drugs or else they're drunk the whole time. How can you suggest a boy that age should see more of them?'

Edith, taken aback by Alfred's vehemence, said, 'I wasn't suggesting he saw more of them. But if I'd said he should never see them again he wouldn't have paid any attention. You have to work with the realities of the situation. I'd have thought you'd have been more sympathetic. After all, you had your own hippy phase.'

'That was completely different. In the first place it was cheerful. It was a way of living more simply, a sort of pastoral thing if you like, not a miserable collapse into nihilism. We thought people would see the point and become more like us, we didn't hate them, like this lot do, droning on about how they hate the system, pretending to be poor when the system gives them enough for an Indian family to live on for a year.'

'I didn't know you felt so strongly.'

'I've seen these people, we had two hundred of them on John Jarrett's doorstep for over a year before they could be turned off. You've never seen such filth as they left behind.'

'I know. Of course. But as a matter of fact I do know a bit about them too. They're the same people I used to come across as squatters when I was a magistrate in London. There are different sorts. You start at the gentle hippy-ish end of the spectrum and go on through the harmless inadequates to the brutish small-time criminal end. And when they start hugging trees, that's good, that's a development. They may get really interested and meet other sorts of people and find out how decisions get made. Something may come of it. Sean may go on, if he's got any intelligence, which I don't know that he has.'

'Go on with what? A career of law-breaking?'

'Perhaps a career of trying to get things done without breaking the law.'

'That seems extraordinarily optimistic.'

'I believe in being extraordinarily optimistic. I always have.'

'And some of your swans, as I remember, have turned into geese.'

'I'm not saying he's a swan . . .' But Alfred had left the room, rather hunched; Edith heard him slowly climbing the stairs.

'Crosspatch,' said Edith.

'Dear Moley,' Alfred had written in the holidays. 'My sister is always trying to get me to go to singing practice. There is this pageant they are putting on. She likes going round to all the different places. They go in a bus and then they sing. There is a toad by the kitchen steps. I suppose he lives there. He can blow himself up when he is angry but not very much but still he does it to the utmost of his capacity.'

Alfred used to go with his mother out of the kitchen door, past the toad (who only came out in the evenings) and up the hill. Sometimes, when Edith and her father had gone on one of the more distant choir outings, they took their lunch and walked all day. They went quite slowly because there were so many things to stop and look at. Sometimes as they went his mother talked to him about India, about the birds and plants and animals there, and about the people who had looked after her when she was a small child and about how much she missed them, even now. She told him that her father had taught her about Indian birds, because he used to makes notes about them wherever he went and send them to a friend of his who lived somewhere in the hills to the north and who was making a list of all the birds of India and all their different habitats. So when she had been sent to England when she was thirteen to go to a boarding school, she had comforted herself in her loneliness by learning about all the English birds. In time she came to know their different songs as well. She found her school strict and cold, but there had been a teacher called Miss Murphy who had been kind to her when she had discovered her interest in natural history. Miss Murphy had been the classics mistress, and though Janet Ashby had studied neither Latin nor Greek, having had enough trouble with English Literature and Mathematics and Biology, Miss Murphy had sometimes talked to her when she was sitting by herself in the garden (because it took her a long time to make any friends among girls with whom at first she had little in common). Miss Murphy had told her about how love of the beauty of the natural world could lead you on to love divine beauty, and she had not minded when the girl had said that she thought she would leave divine beauty until later, but had laughed and said, 'One day you will read all this in Plato.' Telling this to her young son, Janet had said that she never had read Plato, but Alfred knew that she had not needed to, because this thought was natural to her, and the wellspring of her being.

Arthur Ashby walked every day 'up and round' with Pibroch the cairn, but he was not interested in toads or birds or trees. Only Alfred shared his mother's love of the natural world and only Alfred knew how in that love was the true depth and intensity of her being. Since her death he had not been able to think of her hands cupped round a caterpillar on a leaf, held out to show him, her long fingers square-ended, stained with grass, or her touch on his arm as she pointed to the bright flash of a kingfisher on the lower reaches of the stream, or the delight on her face when they watched the dippers swimming under water higher up, in the little pools under the trees, without feeling that there was a sense in which he alone had known her. It had left him with a feeling, which he had never quite been able to examine, that he had failed her. She had made him understand what to her was the most important thing in the world, and he had kept it to himself, whereas perhaps it was something which he should have built upon, or at least passed on. Or was it just that, sharing this knowledge as he did, he of all people ought to have been with her when she died? He thought of her at least once nearly every day, and each time with a quick flash of pain. There it was, a mark he carried with him.

'Alfred thinks I ought to marry Hubert,' wrote Edith to Jeannie.

I can't think why. I have been married twice already and my present arrangement suits me admirably. It suits Hubert too. He can spend as much time as he likes gossiping with other journalists without thinking he ought to be at home with the wife. He used to ask me to marry him from time to time, but he's given up lately. It was after his wife died, and I suppose he was used to being married even though it hadn't been much fun for years. His wife had muscular dystrophy, you know, and was in a wheelchair. She had a sharp tongue and wasn't easy to look after. She was an Irish journalist, protégée of Lord Beaverbrook, witty and dashing and all that, but when struck down by the disease I believe she was foul to poor old Hubert. Not that he told me, other people did. We used to meet for lunch to talk about politics, and one day when I asked him what he'd wanted to talk about he said, 'Nothing really, I just wanted to bask,' and then he sang, 'You are my sunshine, my only sunshine,' (he'd had a glass or two of wine by then) and the absurdly camp waiter who was pouring the coffee said, 'My absolute fave,' which rather put Hubert off his stride. Well, of course I am fond of him, it's a long friendship – we didn't become lovers until after his wife died – and he saw me through that time after Derek when I used to wake up every morning with a sense of doom and had to battle with the bad publicity and a press which wouldn't believe I hadn't known about Derek's tricks. Then there was the lost election, and the party destroying itself with stupid rows about procedure, and me just not having the faith in myself to bang their heads together as I should have done. Of course, Sarah saved me first of all, as she always has, by understanding everything, but also by needing me, and then it was you, because you suggested I should teach English to your refugees and after that the language school just grew of itself. But I did come to depend quite a bit on Hubert, and I think he liked that because I suppose he was sort of in love with me, which I had no idea of at the time. Anyway, he's a good old friend, but we don't need to get married. And besides he smokes too much.

In fact Edith would have liked to ask Hubert's advice about Sarah; Alfred was right about that. She could not explain to Alfred that she had resolved not to communicate with Hubert during the time she spent in the country because she was not quite sure herself, without going into the whole question more deeply than she cared to do, why it had seemed such a good idea. As a result she was more annoyed with Alfred about his attitude towards her remarks to Sean Jupp than was perhaps warranted in view of the fact that she already knew how much he disliked the travellers. She decided to do some cooking. Perhaps Alfred would be in a better mood by lunchtime.

It was Derek who had taught her most of what she knew about cooking. She had known the rudiments of course, and had made her own discoveries by trial and error during her marriage to Johnny, but until she met Derek her only guide had been the 1954 *Good Housekeeping Cookery Book* which she had been given by Caroline Cornish as a wedding present, and even that she seldom bothered to consult. She and Johnny lived on sausages and mash and shepherd's pie and when they had people to dinner she did a chicken casserole; her lemon meringue pie was popular, but apart from the whipped cream it came out of a packet. The first time she and Derek had breakfast together in her house, he told her that eggs should be scrambled in a *bain-marie* and when he had explained that that meant a double saucepan and discovered that she did not possess such a thing, he took it on himself to re-equip her kitchen and to introduce her to Elizabeth David's *French Provincial Cooking*. He had a few exotic extras of his own invention, including a dish involving a whole cotechino sausage, a handful of juniper berries and half a bottle of vintage port which Edith herself secretly never thought a total success, but he gave her a new understanding of the whole subject of food and its presentation, and there were many little rules which she acquired at that time and never broke thereafter. She always tossed rice in hot olive oil before boiling it, added chocolate and blackcurrant jam to oxtail stew, and crushed the carcass to add to the sauce for tarragon chicken. The fact remained that she was not an instinctive cook, and she recognized that Hubert, a much simpler and certainly neater cook than Derek, was a better one than she was. As to why she seemed to prefer men who took an unusual interest in food (and had a consequent tendency to get fat), she could not guess; even Johnny had always been what he called a good trencherman.

Edith peeled some onions, then opened the drawer in the kitchen table and found the curved chopping implement with two handles which she and Derek had bought in the market in Alfred's local village on their visit to Italy. Derek was in Peru, for all she knew, teaching some dark-haired sophisticate the recipe for cotechino sausage with junipers and port; or was he in Guatemala, admiring local cooking utensils in some remote forest settlement, bearded perhaps, gone to seed, alone?

The thought of Derek alone was curiously alarming; it always had been. Derek alone might be a stranger; not the master of his world after all, but an angry fighter of losing battles, struggling to impose his fantasy on facts which would not submit to being shouted at. Edith had always known that

Derek alone might be a little mad; she had chosen not to think about it. He had not been mad when he had taken over her political campaign, only inexhaustible, and unexpectedly tactful. Those few of her party who were initially suspicious were soon seduced. Graham the school-teacher, who suspected Derek of being a businessman, which in his eyes was worse than being a Marxist or a Fascist because it made some people richer than others – a view which Derek would normally have treated with loud derision – was treated to a lecture about Government policy for the disabled (Derek's firm having once been employed as consultants by a private charity working in that field) which left him with the impression that altruism had at last become a force in British politics and that Derek himself was probably a saint. Even Jeannie Mackintosh, to whom Derek was always a joke, thought him a wonderful joke, and Betty Mainwaring, who was indefatigable at putting leaflets into envelopes but was otherwise not Edith's favourite among her followers, made it only too clear that she would have preferred Derek to have been the candidate rather than Edith.

Jeannie, splendidly pregnant in a saffron robe, dropped into the committee rooms with a folio of her husband Max's architectural drawings under her arm and a number of very small children in her wake. She had been embarrassing the art gallery up the road by suggesting they put on an exhibition of Max's work (Max himself would have been even more embarrassed had he known anything about it) and half the children were orphans from Vietnam. She brought her usual atmosphere of dauntless optimism; as usual, too, her comments were surprisingly to the point.

'You know what,' she said. 'Your Derek. He's going to sweep the Independent Citizens Party to victory, there's no doubt about that. You're going to be in Parliament, head of a new party, a public figure. You'll have to think of what to do about your organization. We're all much too amateur except for Derek. After you've won, after the euphoria, everyone's going to start quarrelling. You ought to make Derek Chairman of the Party and get him to think about how he's going to run it. That's if you're really going to go on in the way he obviously thinks you are. Myself, I'd like you just to be a rogue MP causing trouble and raising awkward questions, but I don't think that's what Derek envisages.'

'I'm not quite sure what Derek envisages. He lives for the moment more than you might think.'

'What will he do when you're in Parliament and he's left at home?'

'He'll be relieved, I should think. He's had to give up an awful lot of time to all this. He's got masses of his own work to do.'

His own work, however, soon changed its nature. Edith was never quite sure whether it had been the amount of time he had had to spend on her affairs which soured his relations with his colleagues, or whether there had been some deeper cause. It even occurred to her afterwards that they might have used his frequent absences as an excuse to bring the situation to a head; there seemed to be a lot of old scores to be settled. Old scores and old expense accounts, as far as Edith could make out; some of it sounded very petty. Derek did not want to talk about it. He stumped up and down their small drawing-room with his peculiar rolling gait, fulminating indistinctly and calling them all shits; but after a time he washed his hands of it, accepted some minimal compensation and moved on to the next thing, which was property. He had bought a terrace of houses on the borders of Chelsea and Fulham in the early sixties. They had been due for demolition and then somehow they had not been demolished, and eventually he had rebuilt and refurbished them and made a comfortable profit from selling the leases. He had been doing the same sort of thing in a quiet way ever since. Now he expanded into commercial property and undeveloped land, and for a time things went swimmingly. There was a rather grand office not far from Hyde Park Corner, and a car and a driver to collect him from home every morning. Edith was busy with her new Parliamentary life and delighted that he was busy and successful too. Before Sarah went to boarding-school, the car and the driver used to drop her off at her London day school, and collect her again in the afternoons. It was a good time. When Edith first noticed a kind of speeding-up in Derek's life, an occasional feverishness in his intense activity, she thought the answer might be that they needed more holidays. They planned to go to Italy again, and stay with Alfred, but the time never seemed to be right. In what Edith later realized must have been a defensive reaction to the increasingly bad news on the property front, Derek threw himself into more and more occupations. He took on a few accounts from his old business, loyal clients who wanted him to go on handling their publicity. It led to further disagreements with his ex-colleagues. Then he had some involvement with a man he had known in the war who thought the country was on the point of collapse and was in the process of getting together what seemed to be a private army, to be ready to defend the constitution. He knew that Edith was, to put it mildly, sceptical as to the usefulness of this endeavour, so he claimed not to take it seriously; but it was one more cause for long telephone calls and late-night meetings. Edith, busy herself, did not seek to know more than he told her; they seemed to have such a tremendous lot to talk about, anyway. In those first years of their marriage – in all the years of their marriage really, until near the end – Edith questioned very little. For the first time in her life, sense, emotion and reason were all satisfied, her doubts were stilled, her cravings quiet, her ambition satisfied. She aban-doned herself to Derek; generous in love, he gave her back herself as she had always wanted to be, confident and com-petent. He said he had never had anyone to love. They were his loved ones, he said, she and Sarah. 'How have they been today, my loved ones?' He showered them with presents, amused them with his tales of high life, made them a conspiracy of three to reap the world's available benefits. There was nothing they could not do, he implied, with a little ingenuity, a bold approach, a car and a driver.

That was why, when things began to go wrong, Edith took so long to notice; she had suspended her critical faculty, as far as Derek was concerned. Afterwards she thought that if Sarah had been there things might have been different; but Sarah was by then at boarding-school. By the time Edith suddenly sat up in bed one day and said, 'But, Derek, people don't do things like that,' it was too late; the bit was between his teeth. That was the morning he appeared to be proposing to rob a bank. Lloyds Bank in the King's Road was holding the title deeds to some houses which he had not been able to sell, owing to the sudden slump in property; the bank was refusing to release them until he paid off his overdraft.

'You'd be surprised,' he said, 'the things people do.'

He was stumping up and down the bedroom in his silk pyjamas, his face pink and a little puffy from sleep, his ruffled greyish hair standing up rather comically from his head. They had been woken early by a telephone call from a man called Spencer Broadleas who was some kind of expert on mortgages. Edith had met him on various occasions when he had come to the house. He had a military air, like so many of Derek's associates, and wore a dark business suit and carried an expensive briefcase, but Edith found it disconcerting that he seemed unable to meet her eye when he replied to her friendly greetings. When she mentioned this to Derek he said breezily, 'He had a spot of bother, had to go inside for a month or two. It always affects them like that. Something to do with an export licence.'

Derek had clearly been upset by the early-morning telephone call. He answered angrily, issuing rapid instructions which were incomprehensible to Edith and evidently unwelcome to Spencer Broadleas.

'Oh, yes,' he said afterwards, still agitated, 'I could tell you a thing or two about what people do. And get away with. I know all about it. I know people who can get me anything I want. Rub people out too, no problem.'

'Derek, do go and have your bath.'

After his bath he was calm again. He told her he hated being woken up by the telephone, that was all, she was not to worry, people were silly and got over-excited but everything was under control. It was summer, and hot in London. Derek wore what he called his white ducks – canvas trousers which he hitched up with a belt rather high over his stomach, and a white shirt which he sometimes changed twice a day because he said it didn't matter a man being fat as long as he didn't look sweaty, an ambition he did not always achieve. He seemed forever on the move, too busy to meet her for lunch or dinner in the House of Commons, often out in the evening when she came home, even when it was after midnight. The busier he became, the faster he walked up and down, sometimes in preoccupied silence, sometimes talking, often carrying the telephone on the special long flex he had had installed. Then he would put the telephone down on the nearest piece of furniture and almost inevitably trip over the flex in the course of further pacing; then he would turn scarlet with rage and shout incoherently. Edith anxiously tried to calm him, saying he would make himself ill; that made him even angrier.

'You should support me. Serious matters. You should be helping me expose these criminals.'

'I will if you tell me who they are. You don't tell me. Is it the banks?'

'Banks, insurance companies, criminal conspiracy, oh yes. You know they're watching this house.'

'Derek, wait, please. Of course I have faith in you, of course I believe you, but this is paranoia, you're letting things get on top of you. Just tell me and let me help you.'

'Got to keep you out of it, nothing to do with you. I'll tell you this, though. That friend of yours, Inman. You remember Inman? He's in this, he's a shifty bugger if ever there was one.'

'You mean that awful Lord you tried to palm me off with when we first met? He's your friend, not mine. What's he done?'

'Was my friend. Was my friend. Owes me a lot, that man. I got him his job, made him a lot of money. What does he do? Drops me, drops me like a hot potato when things get rough. He could have supported me with the bank, his bloody great firm could have stood behind me, and now what? He's in a meeting. Yesterday, today, tomorrow, he's in a meeting. Ha. I'll ditch him. I know a thing or two.'

'Not revenge, Derek. Revenge is never worth it, honestly.'

'This won't be revenge, it'll get me out of hock, that's all. I owe him nothing now. He's been investing in Spain, holiday complexes, all very fine and above board, American co-investors, shares booming, I can sell at the top of the market.'

'That's wonderful. Have you got a lot of shares?'

'None. I'll go short. When the time comes. When I'm sure of my sources. If there's one thing I've still got, it's sources.' He gave a sudden shout of laughter, good humour restored. Edith, relieved, asked no more questions. She could not bear it when his mood was black. She suspected him of provoking quarrels with her so that he could release his rage, which was not against her but against the world. He would unexpectedly take offence at something she said, become furious, unreasonable; she responded indignantly, never learning patience, and only ended the argument by going to bed. In the morning she suffered his reproaches, then his remorse, then his self-pity. 'You must be nice to me, you must support me.' Then he would want to make love, but his greed for consolation distressed her; the joy had gone out of his urgency, and though she submitted to it she bit her hand to stop her mouth, lest she should say aloud that he disgusted her. In the daytime she tried to concentrate on her work, telling herself that everything would be all right when the Parliamentary recess came, when they could go away, when Sarah came home from school.

Afterwards it occurred to her that he might have had another reason for provoking quarrels. He might have wanted her to want him to leave. It could have been his last kindness to her. In the end he went very suddenly, time having run out. She came home from the House of Commons one Monday evening, after a terrible weekend, to find a policeman on her doorstep and a letter from Derek on her desk. The weekend had been terrible because the Government seemed about to collapse and there were countless telephone calls about election plans, and because Derek had apparently gone mad. He had been up very early on Friday morning and had gone out to buy the *Daily Mail* and the *Financial Times*. When he had read them, he began to shout and swear and telephone and pace up and down with his jerky step, pulling up his white trousers higher and higher until there was a good six inches of white sock showing below them above his brown and white golfing shoes. Then he dashed from the house. After that she saw him only when he rushed in and out on two or three occasions to collect papers, and on one occasion clothes; she did not know where he slept. When she tried to speak to him he said, 'Shut up, shut up, you're finished now, that's all over, all over, d'you see?' She watched him helplessly from the doorstep, his strange seafaring gait taking him away from her into the traffic.

'You will realize I have been worried,' he had written.

Well, they've got me, I'm afraid. My debts are huge and I've cut a few corners. I told you nothing about any of it because there was no way in which you could help. We have been getting on badly for some time and I expect you will be glad to be rid of me. Don't try and find me, I'm going much too far for that. I expect you to divorce me as soon as possible and have left a letter with my lawyer to that effect. As you know I admire your public work immensely and know you will continue with that. Best wishes.

This letter seemed to her cruel; she wept. The policeman, who had accompanied her into the house, asked about the letter; she held it out to him. In the end the police believed her when she said she knew nothing more; it took longer for the press to lose interest. The investigations into Derek's affairs dragged on interminably; Edith tried to avoid knowing the outcome. Mortgage fraud, impropriety over share dealings, cheating the Inland Revenue and the banks – what good did it do to tell her all that now? The week of Derek's disappearance saw another scandal break in the newspapers. It seemed that Lord Inman and his fellow directors had known for some time that their American co-investors in Spanish holiday homes were withdrawing from the scheme. Inman and one other director had been quietly disposing of their shares. The news broke before they were ready for it, and they lost a lot of money. Inman was threatened with prosecution, but the case eventually faded out for lack of evidence, though according to Stock Exchange regulations he was never again allowed to become a director of a public company. It appeared that someone had been selling massively just before the disclosure; the shares duly plummeted at the news, but the unknown investor, who had clearly intended to buy at the bottom of the market the shares he had already sold at the top, had had bad luck. Mr Heath's decision to call a general election pushed the news out of the newspapers; it broke the following week, by which time dealings in the shares had been suspended. The speculator was left with a huge debt and a number of awkward questions unanswered. In due course Edith understood that this unlucky investment had been Derek's last throw.

There were two other letters. She found them on her pillow. One was addressed to Edith and Sarah.

That other letter was in case you had to show it to anyone. This is just for you two. I've gone bust, also committed a few irregularities in trying to avoid it (actually made it worse). It's not as bad for me as it would be for some, I've always lived a bit on the edge. I've known for a long time how to disappear if need be, so DON'T TRY AND FIND ME. You don't have to quite forget me, only enough not to feel sad. I didn't deserve you, but I did love you. You were far and away the best thing that ever happened to me or ever could happen. In the regiment I was known as a hairy heel, good man but a bit of a hairy heel. Well, now I'm kicking up my hairy heels and making off. Be your dear selves and NO REGRETS – promise, D.

The other letter, which was addressed to Edith only, simply said, 'SORRY, OLD THING, xxxxxxxxx'

She had to make do with that.

Alfred walked restlessly from room to room, bored by his photographs, which were too familiar to him. He would have liked to go downstairs but wanted to keep out of the way of Edith in case she started to lecture him about something. Not having seen her for some time, he had forgotten, as he always did, quite how bossy she was. He recognized that she was often right; it was not that, it was that she went on about things so. Of course she had done some good now and then – quite a lot of good, perhaps, which was more than he could say of himself. She had worked with the grain of her temperament, which was active, and in some ways high-handed. Had not their father done the same, and for that matter their grandfather on the other side, their mother's father, so what could be expected? He had no right to feel irritated by her, and no need to feel a kind of embarrassed pain for her either, as if he were obliged by their sibling relationship to offer himself as a substitute to be bruised on her behalf.

He had found this grandfather's house one day in Simla. He had been photographing the Lakkar Bazaar for the Japanese travel magazine for which he often worked and had wandered on up the hillside and seen through an overgrown gateway a pinnacled ruin which invited exploration. The chain which held the iron gate closed had rusted through and, pushing it open, he saw on the grassy drive a young bullock calf which looked at him uneasily and edged past him back towards the gate. Uncertain where the calf belonged, Alfred gave the gate a slight push; the calf, evidently expecting this, butted it fully open with its head and trotted out on to the roadway, where a young boy with a stick shouted at it and the two of them proceeded down the hill. Hoping not to be intercepted by a furious property owner now deprived of his calf, Alfred walked cautiously up the drive and past rampant vegetation to reach a circle of weed-infested gravel and the ruin, a good deal smaller than he had supposed, of a villa only a little more fanciful than the average Saracenic-Victorian hybrid which had already charmed him in Simla. A party of monkeys on the roof of the conservatory turned tail at his approach and scattered noisily, dislodging a pane of glass, which shattered on the tiled floor. Double doors swung on their hinges; walking in, Alfred saw that at least half of the glass was similarly spread about on the floor, whose Puginesque tiles seemed still as good as new and reminded him forcibly of the long back passages of his preparatory school in the Malvern hills. The main entrance to the house seemed, unusually, to be through this conservatory which fronted the whole building in a narrow serpentine curve, the broadest section of which had room for a tall lead fountain, now tipped at an irrational angle over its dry alabaster basin. He tried the door into the house but found it locked. Outside he found that a large unfinished concrete building immediately adjoined the house on the other side from the drive; no work seemed to be in progress. Walking round it, he came upon what must once have been the view from the house, a wooded downward slope, a nearby hill with houses among its trees, and beyond that mountains, increasing in height and extending into the far distance, culminating in the long line of white peaks which were the remote Himalayas.

156

Beyond the unfinished concrete block Alfred found a small, dismal hotel, where a sleeping porter woke reluctantly to tell him the ruined house belonged to a man who lived in Bombay and was going to do it up; if Alfred wanted to see inside, he could get him a key the next day. Idly curious, Alfred returned the following morning and was shown one unexpectedly large room lined with a number of flimsy upright chairs.

'Ballroom,' the man said.

The only other room to which he had access was a little dark room on the ground floor opening out on to a verandah and a close view of the building next door.

'Master bedroom,' he said.

It was the oddity of the conservatory and the ballroom which interested Alfred enough to send him to the various books about Simla which he had found in the excellent bookshop in the Mall, and there he discovered to his surprise that the house had belonged to his grandfather and had been enlarged by him in the 1880s, supposedly in the hope that it might be bought by the Government, since the existing viceregal lodge was considered too small and possibly unhealthy in view of the numbers of ADCs who had died of dysentery (the house was built over an old graveyard). This hope proved unfounded when Lord Dufferin caused a much grander edifice to be built in 1888.

This then had been for six months of several succeeding years his mother's childhood paradise. Alfred went back to the house once more before he left to return to Delhi, but wandering round the wrecked conservatory or trying to exclude the intrusive concrete block in the garden from his view of the mountains he could evoke no echo. Only later, looking at his photographs, did he find he could impose on them an imaginary past which might or might not have borne some relation to what had once been; the child in the white dress among the exotic carefully tended plants, the authoritarian father benignly amused by her pet monkey, the mother faint in the heat holding out a hand to take a cool drink from the silver tray held by the inclining manservant; the child's laughter, sitting golden-haired in a basket saddle on the narrow back of a mountain pony, led by a red-turbaned groom and accompanied on foot by a dark-skinned nurse from the southern state where she had been born, who walked beside her with a proud and tender smile. Perhaps they passed a hurrying messenger with a letter from the Viceroy, to be handed from servant to servant until the father, opening it, gave peremptory orders, as a result of which horses were brought and he rode away, confident of his convictions, his ability to command, his imperial purpose. Alfred had never met this grandfather, who had died soon after his retirement, bored by England and inactivity, but he remembered the widowed grandmother, a spirited old woman who never referred to her life in India except occasionally to look up from her tapestry at the mention of some name and say, 'Terrible people, we knew them in India.' Perhaps it had been a man's world; or a child's.

'Sir Cuthbert was indefatigable in his concern for the peasant cultivator,' Alfred read, 'though not all the schemes proceeding from his fertile mind met with equal success.' And in the photographs he did look rather like Edith; the same broad cheeks and big blue eyes, the same firm chin and confident bearing. So there maybe she had been half a century later, knowing best and organizing people, galvanizing some, irritating others, no more mistaken or resented or misunderstood than he had been, but without his power. This power had invested him with such majesty in the eyes of his daughter Janet that she had never in her life supposed it possible for a woman, or an Indian, to be other than an underling. In the case of his granddaughter Edith, on the other hand, who had never known him and hardly ever thought about him, it might have been an unconscious inheritance, a seed of mustard in the blood.

'Well, Edith,' said Alfred, coming downstairs in much better humour, 'you'd have made a fine colonial governor.'

13

'I've made a few inquiries,' said Charlie Warburton, leaning closer to Edith so as not to be overheard. 'I think we might be able to get that track reclassified without attracting any attention.'

There were only three other people in the pub, apart from Mrs Hurley the proprietress who was reading a Mills and Boon novel behind the bar. There was a young couple who were interested only in each other and an old man who was dozing by the fire. Edith had already noticed that Charlie Warburton enjoyed being conspiratorial.

'Even so, people can appeal, can't they?' she said.

'Always much harder to change things if there's got to be a public inquiry. The expense puts people off.'

'I haven't said anything to Alfred yet. I think if you wanted to make one of the routes go along the valley behind the house he'd never agree to it.'

'We'd only do that occasionally. It would be the absolute top thrill, sort of thing. A couple of times a year, no more. And if we were the organizers we'd be in control, we'd never have people wandering in unofficially, don't you see? I say, incidentally, what does he do about insurance?'

'What sort of insurance?'

'Building fabric, all that sort of thing. Walls, he's got a lot of wall, hasn't he? Gets a bit of frost damage, I've no doubt, in a winter like this. I can put him in touch with an excellent firm if he wants me to, they specialize in this sort of thing, historic buildings and so on, they give very good rates to friends of mine. Shall I get them to drop him a line?'

'If you like. Does Johnny insure with your people?'

He laughed. 'Good old Johnny. Mean as Croesus, always has been.'

'It's rich as Croesus, surely. Mean as – I don't know – Scrooge?'

'He used to be rich as Croesus, anyway. As well as mean as Scrooge. Until Lloyd's got him, poor chap. Terrible thing that. Total breakdown of morality. Used to be run by honest fools, then they let the clever people in and the whole thing went to pot. Ruined the English counties, of course. No JPs, no charity workers, no meals on wheels. All the gentry are out trying to make a living selling cosmetics on commission, or handiworks; you know, beaded belts like Red Indians. Pathetic.'

'Hermione's going to breed dogs.'

'There you are, then. Killed by their own side. Survived all those Labour governments and their wealth taxes, scuppered by one of their own sacred cows. It's a cruel world.'

'Scuppered by a cow,' said Edith. 'Cruel indeed.'

'I don't think you take me seriously,' said Charles Warburton, looking hurt.

'I do. It's just that the way you put things makes me laugh.'

'I wish we could work together,' said Charles, cheering up. 'We'd get on tremendously well, you know. I'd be jolly good with your students, too. I could take them on survival courses.'

Alfred, walking in his loden overcoat across the frozen field with a tin of mince pies for Lawrence Raven, wondered why Edith had been so annoyed at the thought of marrying in search of companionship in old age. He suspected that she was unwilling to think about old age at all. Marrying for companionship during the descent into senility seemed very reasonable to him, though he had been for so long without a permanent companion that he felt no such need himself. He might have married once for love, and would have willingly submitted to whatever iron discipline that endeavour might have required from him. He would have done it well; he might even have made some kind of private triumph of it. Deprived of that opportunity, he had not sought another; it had had its painful aspects. Casual affairs on his travels had introduced him to some lovable girls, but he had not pretended to love them; some horrors as well of course, like dreadful Deirdre in her tartan shorts on a bicycle in Provence. Raffaella had been a good creature, though, who had made him go back to St David's. Arriving at Lawrence Raven's front door, he said as Lawrence opened it, 'I was just thinking of St David's. I must go there again some time.'

Lawrence's face broke into smiles of welcome and pleasure. 'Go in the spring, there's no one much about. May's good because of the wild flowers. What's this you've brought? Mince pies? That's very kind.'

'Edith made them. She's been doing a lot of cooking.'

'I thought it might have been you. Back to the days of Alfred's Cakes.'

'I never made them myself, I'm afraid. It was Edwina, Augustine's wife.'

'What happened to those two? Come in, I've just lit the fire. I suppose it's too hot, they've given me this frightful central heating which I can't turn down, but I'm jolly well going to have a fire as well. Is he still a tycoon? I don't seem to read about him in the papers as much as I used to.'

'He's so rich now he's bought total privacy. He's married to a smart American lady who organizes a life of hushed luxury for him in their houses in London and New York and Virginia and the West Indies and Provence and anywhere else you like. She gives tremendously grand balls for Aids charities at which he appears for ten minutes and then is driven home in the Rolls to do some more juggling on the currency markets.'

'Do you ever see him?'

'Occasionally. He's got smaller somehow – very neat and precise and well-preserved. He likes the comforts of wealth but he's not interested in the power. That's unusual, I suppose. You couldn't say that wealth has corrupted him. He just likes playing with money.'

'So he's happy?'

'I think so. His conversation's quite boring, but I don't suppose that bothers him. It doesn't bother his wife, either.'

Lawrence settled himself comfortably in his chair by the fire, opened the tin, took a mince pie and put the tin on a conveniently placed stool between his chair and the one on the other side of the fireplace which he had indicated to Alfred.

'And what happened to Muffy?' he said.

'Muffy?'

'The wife.'

'She was called Edwina.'

'I could have sworn it was Muffy. I know there was a Muffy about somewhere. It will come back to me. What happened to Edwina?'

'She runs a rehabilitation centre for drug addicts in Tuscany.'

'Drugs, oh dear. I thought alcohol was her problem.'

'She went a bit off the rails generally at one time. I found them a house near me when I was living in Italy. It was a lovely place, a hamlet on top of a hill which had been a big farm, with lots of outbuildings, miles from anywhere. They restored it rather well, without spoiling it at all, and then they filled it up with all their friends from England. Friends and hangers-on, I suppose.'

Alfred thought of the place with a sudden nostalgia. It had been a fit site for a perfect way of life; they had let it all go, those people. Perhaps he would have done no better himself. As for Augustine, even if he had cared there had not been much he could have done short of throwing them all out, and that would hardly have been his style.

'Things went rather to pieces,' he went on. 'Edwina was out of her head on heroin most of the time, and then she fell in with a sort of witch woman who had a cult not far away. That's when Augustine divorced her, because she was giving away his money. He let her have the house and she used to go back there between drug cures, but she neglected it terribly and the Red Brigade started using it and there was a shoot-out with the carabinieri and all sorts of dramas. That's what pulled her round really, because she didn't want to lose the house. So she stuck to the cure and now she lives there and rehabilitates people. Bells, you know, and dance.'

'Bell, book and candle,' said Lawrence, nodding.

'Tibetan bells. American dance.'

'Same sort of thing, I expect. I've remembered who Muffy was. She was the friend of the young man Lydia threw out in the end.'

'Marigold. Wasn't she called Marigold? Marilyn, perhaps.'

'I knew her as Muffy.'

'Really, Lawrence? Well I've no idea what happened to her, I'm afraid.'

'Happy times,' said Lawrence. 'What about a quick game of chess before you go back? It's much too unpleasant outside to do anything useful.'

There were certain corners of St David's and the part of Pembrokeshire which surrounds it which seemed to linger on the outskirts of Alfred's consciousness and to appear often in his dreams, perhaps every night, except that he did not always remember – just the stone wall by the shallow stream near where the bridge crossed from the churchyard to the path which led up the hill past the ruins of the Bishop's palace, or a not particularly interesting piece of road with grass beside it just before the turning which led to the cliffs by St Non's chapel. He could think of no reason why these places should have imprinted themselves on his mind. When he thought about St David's consciously, he thought of the view over the cathedral and the rooks and pigeons he used to watch every morning.

He had gone back there in September, two and a half years after Lydia's death. He had been out of the country, mainly in Italy, for most of the intervening period, having left as soon as he understood that Nijinsky the black whippet would be as happy with John Jarrett as with him. There was work for him on Italian magazines, and after a year he asked Augustine to help him sell the rest of his shares in the business of Alfred's Emporium (which was then transmuted into Emporium Enterprises, Augustine's apotheosis) and transfer enough of the proceeds to Italy so that he could buy for £3,000 a semi-ruined farmhouse and some land. It was Raffaella who in due course told him he ought to make more effort to look after his vines and olives, and Raffaella who when eventually she knew the story said, 'You have to return to this place where she jumped, you cannot absorb it if you go into hiding.'

He had followed her advice without enthusiasm, thinking there might be quite a lot to be said for remaining in hiding, but, having said he would go, he stuck it out for the two weeks Raffaella had said were essential. Or almost two weeks; on the twelfth day he had known it would be all right to leave. The thing he most remembered was the morning flight and cross-flight of the rooks and the pigeons over the bowl of the green valley in which the ancient cathedral stood, and how the small golden flags on the pinnacles of the cathedral tower were struck by the light of the rising sun at just that time. He would stand at the window of the room he had taken in a cottage which overlooked the churchyard and watch the performance every morning. Then he would drink a cup of tea, and then he would walk down the steep slope to morning prayer. In the evening, in order to impose a structure on his day, he would go to evening prayer. After evening prayer the organist would continue to play; Alfred would sit, often alone, until he finished. On one of these evenings there came into his mind, wiped clean as it seemed to have been by the total immersion in the music with which his concentration had been rewarded, the conviction that Raffaella had been wrong in saying that his photography ought to have a political purpose. He had been on the way to agreeing with her, but now it came to him in the silence after the music that he wanted it to have no purpose at all. This seemed an ideal worthy of his utmost dedication.

The organist was trying to re-invigorate the choir. It was weak in the treble section; boy sopranos must have chanced to be hard to come by in the little town at just that time. The full choir, which on Sundays flowed in procession into the nave down a dramatic slope unplanned by the original build-ers but brought about by subsequent shifts in the soil beneath the cathedral, was strong in the men's section, less effective in the higher reaches. During the weekday services, which were poorly if at all attended, the organist was training a new girls' choir. Alfred would see them flying down the hill on their bicycles after school, and only a few minutes later they would be washed and tidy in their surplices, with serious faces looking across at each other for reassurance as they struck their quiet harmonies. Sometimes they would be supported by the men's voices, and then their ambition knew no bounds. Long and complicated anthems, not always perfectly ex-ecuted, would give Alfred time to drift into entirely peaceful reverie, from which he would emerge with little memory of the music. His thoughts wandered in this way one evening vaguely around the composer's name (was Samuel Sebastian Wesley the son of John Wesley, or the nephew, or the grandson? – he must look him up some day), and the earnest-faced girls whose rounded Welsh vowels so pleased him sang on vigorously with the men supporting them, seeming to flow from one kind of anthem to another, or perhaps it was all the same, and then they were singing alone in a sweet, descending line, 'See that ye love one another,' and then curving up again, 'fervently.' This line was repeated and then repeated and Alfred wept, taken by surprise. But there was no one who knew him, no one who recognized a face connected only with a forgotten death; he could weep if he wanted to, or put his hands together and hold them in front of him like a medieval knight on a tomb, and he could shut his eyes and pray for peace of mind, that the Lord might make His light to shine upon him and give him peace. These things he did, and between morning prayer and evening prayer he walked on the cliffs and round the headland, seeing seals below him and seabirds and sometimes a dashing peregrine, and between evening prayer and morning prayer he dreamed exhaustively, and the fair young man and the dark young man who took it in turns to officiate shook his hand after each service and gently inquired as to his well-being and where he came from, but he answered only as far as politeness required, afraid of finding himself led to admit to these steadfast young men that his adherence to their faith, though not half-hearted, was provisional, metaphorical, and without coherence, and that, moreover, it was likely to remain in that state. By the end of his visit he had not forgiven himself – he never quite did that – but he found to his surprise (because he had not known that it was necessary) that he had forgiven Lydia.

Every evening the rooks settled in the stunted, windswept sycamores between the deanery and the churchyard. Sheltered though they were by the lie of the land from the worst of the gales which came rushing in from the Atlantic, they were often restless on windy nights, setting up a brief cantankerous clatter whenever their branches were unduly agitated. When dawn came after such a night, they seemed especially active. The pigeons which roosted on the massive gateway and bell tower on the top of the slope leading down into the valley in which the small grey cathedral stood, with the ruined Bishop's palace beyond it, seemed to take this extra activity as a challenge. It might be a seagull which first roused them; a whistling cry from high above them they could endure, but if the gulls came lower with their more familiar yapping call, a cloud of pigeons would spiral upwards, circle round and then resettle. When the rooks launched themselves on the first flight of the morning, the reaction was different. The rooks, gleaming black in the pale early light, would dash in a direct diagonal across the churchyard to the cathedral and the trees behind it; the pigeons' response was a rapid flight in close formation along the other diagonal. This flight and counter-flight would accelerate until rooks and pigeons flew together, intersecting like some impossibly speeded-up parade of soldiers marching and counter-marching, while all the time the air through which they rushed brightened with the coming of day, and the cream-coloured stone of the ruins beyond the cathedral seemed to darken as the pale pink wash on the grey stone of the cathedral itself yielded to the clear yellow light which touched upon the yellow of the lichen on the tower. This lichen was the same as that which grew on the outcrop of rock on the hill on the other side of the valley, where the mown fields were the colour of dark straw and the pasture was fawn and pale mauve as well as green. The tournament of the rooks and pigeons lasted until the light was the white light of day and the green in the landscape became the predominant colour after all. Then the birds dispersed, a few rooks remaining to hop and caw prosaically among the jackdaws in the ruins, and a few pigeons hanging plumply about the steps, hoping for the odd crust from a tourist's sandwich.

The exhilaration which Alfred felt when he watched these morning triumphs contributed to his remembering before long that he had things to do himself, which was why he left St David's a few days before the end of the two weeks Raffaella had prescribed for him.

14

Edith wrote to Jeannie:

I like listening to Hubert's gossip, but in fact it isn't true that I'd like to be back in active politics. It's nastier since my day, and politicians haven't learnt how to live with constant press and television harassment, which is much more relentless now; they all sup with the devil and the devil sneaks on them and then they howl. After the way the press persecuted me after Derek disappeared I loathe all newspapers equally but a censored press would be a worse evil, so it just means anyone with any sense avoids the whole circus. Besides, I don't think I am sufficiently partisan. It's just that I can't stand inefficiency. I don't feel violently committed to any particular system, I just want things to work, whether businesses or institutions or committees or anything else, I want them to fulfil their functions and generally get on with it. Only I do understand by now that life's not that simple. When I started I was just carrying on being head prefect. I had quite old-fashioned ideas about how people ought to pull themselves together. I suppose I wanted to improve conditions for the deserving poor, like a Victorian philanthropist, but now I find it's the undeserving poor I sympathize with, the ones who've never quite caught on as to how you get to be deserving, the ones who are too hopeless or too proud to try. That must be something to do with Derek who whatever else he was was hardly priggish.

I suppose what I want is just activity rather than power. That's why I want to expand the school down here. I'm even thinking of entering into partnership with a cheerful idiot who wants to have off-road car rallies. I wanted to involve Sarah but she's obsessed with her own career. She won't even go to Hong Kong with Robert, who's going to work there. It worries me more than I would have believed possible that she should not see how that threatens her family. My example has been so bad. I know I've told you how my mother used to irritate me, but I've come to see just this past week that one of the reasons for that was that she did by her hardly spoken assumptions – and however much I disagreed with her about all sorts of details – leave me with some kind of absolute standard against which to measure myself. I suppose it's that that I've always kicked against. Whereas I don't think I've left Sarah any standards at all. You may say didn't I want her to be independent, have a proper career and all the rest of it – but of course I wanted that AND that she should be a perfect wife and mother – I wanted her to do it all. And if it meant juggling interests and careers at certain times I wanted her to juggle – that's what the New Woman has to be, a judge of priorities, a juggler with needs – which is why her heart needs educating just as much as her brain, and have I perhaps not seen to the education of dear Sarah's heart? You have done so well for your children, because there they are, strong as can be, flourishing with their families in their different parts of the world. I think of them often, five little rocks in a huge stormy sea.

The three roe deer, motionless, their raised heads turned towards Alfred, seemed unusually dark through the white mist and the frost-encrusted branches of the trees, whose trunks, dark too, glistened slightly where the frost had touched them, and showed bare, yellowish wounds where the deer had eaten the bark. Alfred, camera raised, was still too; one of the deer began cautiously to approach him, head forward, ears alert, curious.

The film in the camera wound itself on; she paused at the sound of it. The smaller buck behind her moved away, and the other two followed him, cream-coloured rumps turned towards Alfred. Suddenly all three changed direction and ran back past him, leaping through the silvery undergrowth with springing bounds; Alfred, down on his knees, recorded their passage.

'Well done, John,' he said, as John Jarrett walked slowly towards him through the mist.

'Should have had a gun,' said John.

'Will Mrs Hurley give us a cup of coffee?' said Alfred, picking up his camera case.

The low-ceilinged pub smelt of stale tobacco and beer, but the fire was already lit and Mrs Hurley gave them coffee and large microwaved sausage rolls, and asked John Jarrett whether he knew that the man he had sold his property to was planning to turn it into a race-track. She became indignant when it was clear that neither John nor Alfred believed her.

'I've heard him talking about it. He had a couple of chaps in here from Bristol. They came in those little-four-wheeled drive things like he has, and they were on about the cornering and the hill-climbing and all that. And the bridle paths. You ask your sister, she knows all about it.'

'I know he took her for a drive,' said Alfred. 'She said she was scared out of her wits.'

'You ask her about his plans. They were talking about it, about a club house and tracks radiating out from it all over the place. Could have been that old stockyard opposite you they were going to use.' She glowed with satisfaction at being the bearer of bad news. Alfred, though he knew her pleasure came from love of drama rather than any particular malice, was all the same irritated by the implication that he was not in Edith's confidence.

'He'd never get permission,' he said dampingly.

'He could get the footpaths reclassified,' said Mrs Hurley. 'That's what they do.'

'There've never been four-wheeled vehicles on those tracks,' said John Jarrett. 'You never know, though. There's a field a mile or two away where they do it and they don't half churn up the ground. The noise is something awful, goes on all day.'

'I'll ask Mrs Sainty,' said Alfred. 'She's the expert on all these things. She's bound to know what to do. Remember how good she was when we had the public inquiry about the ski-slope?'

'Tied that inspector in knots. Fine looking woman, too.'

'Quite large,' said Alfred, doubtfully.

'All the better to frighten the planners. If they had their way, there'd be no farming left. We'd import all our food and turn the countryside over to what they call leisure pursuits. Whatever they may be. I never had no leisure pursuits.'

'You watch the telly, don't you?'

'Traditional country pastime that is,' said John Jarrett.

15

In the light of the full moon the large two-storeyed house stood clearly defined at the end of the long drive, isolated from the trees on one side and the shrubbery on the other by a white expanse of frosty grass. The house was white too, stuccoed and porticoed with Regency formality. It had never been a welcoming house, Edith thought, seeing it for the first time in thirty years; but in the moonlight and the frost it had a kind of spare correctness. If she had ever lived there herself she would have been sorry to leave it.

The front door was open, warm golden light spilling out into the icy night air; the sound of many voices came from somewhere within.

'I didn't know it was a party,' said Edith without enthusiasm, leading the way into the stone-flagged hall and adding her coat to the pile thrown over a large oak chest.

'What a night, what a night.' Johnny hurried to greet them, the noise of voices swelling from the room behind him. 'Ten degrees of frost. Full moon, did you see? And the icicles over the porch? Greasy Joan, what? Icicles hang by the pail and so on? Greasy Joan's night off, actually. Hermione's the cook. I'm the butler, what? Look here, it's an absolute nightmare in there. Far too many people. God knows why she's done it again. I thought we'd had the farewell party. Turns out that was just episode one. It's a serial, don't you know? Serial murder, if you ask me. Come in, come in, here's Hermione. I'll just go and put the dogs away, shall I?'

'No, you don't,' shouted Hermione much as if she were talking to one of the dogs. 'Give them champagne. Introduce them.'

'God, yes, drinks. Look here, drinks.'

172

'Don't worry.' Alfred took the bottle of champagne out of Johnny's shaking hand and went to find some glasses.

'Here we are, then,' said Johnny, taking Edith's arm. 'Now you know our dear Lord Lieutenant and his gallant lady, and this is Lorna Molesworth, Hester Banks, Lord and Lady Inman. That'll do to be getting on with. Edith Ashby, my last Duchess, what? Nothing like bad taste to get an evening going. I'll just go and see about those dogs.'

Edith, made aware by his explosive delivery of Johnny's nervousness, amounting almost to panic, shook hands firmly with the people to whom she had been introduced, and began an indeterminate sort of conversation with Hester Banks, a sandy-haired woman about her own age whose face was vaguely familiar; Edith searched her memory in case this might be a re-encounter with the past.

'Needlework,' said Hester Banks. 'The V and A.'

No buried reminiscence stirred. Edith turned instead towards Lady Inman, who was approaching her with a look of amusement on her saturnine features.

'You haven't the faintest idea who I am.'

Edith could only look puzzled.

'Caroline. Caroline Cornish. I've been ill. No one recognizes me these days.'

'Caroline! It's not possible!'

Genuinely astonished, Edith still found time to glance across at Alfred. He was standing by the wall with a glass in each hand and a look of complete disengagement on his face. Edith recognized a situation familiar from perhaps as many as fifty years ago, when they used to come to children's parties in this house. In those days she had uncomplainingly joined in all the games, given up her place in musical chairs when it was wrongly claimed by some other child, and answered nicely whenever a grown-up spoke to her, in order to make up for Alfred's silent non-participation; even then she would be sure to see that he got his fair share of ice-cream and did not leave without his present. This time she would have been glad of her glass of champagne, but for the time being she turned resolutely back to Caroline Cornish, who used to be at those parties too, pretty and self-possessed and spoilt; now she had become strangely masculine in appearance and seemed to have no neck.

'I had terrible kidney trouble, nearly died,' she was saying in her old trumpeting tones. 'Too frightful. You know Peter, don't you? He said he made a pass at you once. We met in a bin. He had ghastly business worries, poor thing, so he took to drink. I was an alcoholic for years. I went to that ghastly commune, d'you remember? It was so boring and so cold there was nothing to do but drink, really. Anyway, happy ending, here we are.'

'How wonderful.'

'Yes, well . . .'

Johnny was suddenly there, leering incomprehensibly and holding out a glass of champagne; she took it and he disappeared with a meaningful wink. Edith drank some champagne and wondered why he was behaving so oddly; but perhaps nowadays he always did. It was of no importance. Disturbed though these waters might be, she could keep afloat; she was no longer young and was not to be intimidated.

'A joke really, isn't it?' said Caroline with her huge toothy smile, which was more alarming now that she seemed so like a man. There was some sort of entreaty in her eyes, and Edith rested a hand lightly on her shoulder for a moment in response. It was probably the first affectionate gesture she had made during the many years of their supposed friendship, which had been more of an intermittent rivalry, really. Of course it was a joke that Caroline should have become this strange person in a white frilled shirt and a long tartan skirt such as she might have worn as a young married woman going out to dinner with country neighbours in the fifties. Ten years later, proprietress of the two most fashionable dress shops in London, she would have greeted such an outfit with shrieks of scornful laughter. Evidently unsure as to how to respond to Edith's gesture, Caroline now raised one hand to fiddle with her pearls, a habit she had always had and which had evidently survived the disappearance of the neck round which the pearls used once to hang; now they seemed to emerge from some infinitesimal space between her ears and her substantial shoulders. The fourth finger of the hand she raised bore on it a large emerald ring; it was as if she were drawing attention to the fact that the man she had married might be neither estimable nor any longer rich but he seemed to have kept some family jewellery, so perhaps the joke had its advantages.

Edith, still smiling, murmured, 'I must just . . .' and plunged into the crowd, making her way in the general direction of Alfred. One or two people glanced at her with a half-smile, as if they were not sure whether or not they might remember her from long ago, but most were concentrating on trying to make themselves heard.

'Frightful skid . . . heating . . . remember the snow in was it sixty-one? . . . kills the germs . . . we always used to skate . . .'

'Failed all her A-levels . . . can't get into Oxford if you went to a public school anyway . . .'

'They go to Thailand in their gap, don't know a thing about Europe . . .'

'We *lived* by the navy, didn't we?' – a frail elderly female voice – 'I mean they protected us, Richard's the last of the family, forcibly retired at only thirty-eight, what will he do? since the 1770s we were a naval family . . .'

'Well, of course until comparatively recently all liabilities were unlimited' – a hearty bass – 'there wasn't such a thing as limited liability, families round here went up and down like anything, bad speculations, ships that didn't come home . . .'

'But these Lloyd's people were crooks, surely? . . .'

'Oh yes, well, always plenty of those about . . .'

'Should have married foreign royalty, some good plain German girl, Lichtenstein or something, trained up to do her duty, they should never have got mixed up with the English upper classes, I said at the time it would be their downfall . . .'

'I thought it was television, their downfall, I mean . . .'

'Downfall of us all, we know too much. All a bit wrong, too. Know too much and all a bit wrong . . .'

'Decent of Hermione, I must say, I'd never have Bill's ex to a party, except the children's weddings of course, but even then they had to put us in separate marquees . . .'

'So interested to hear one of your father's works, an introduction to an orchestral suite, *King Arthur.* I thought it very good, last year's Bath Festival. Are there recordings?'

'Yes,' she answered. 'Mainly of his songs. But they're doing some more, there's a young conductor who's rather keen.'

'They're coming back, composers from his time, aren't they?' said the same long freckled face. Hester Banks, Edith remembered.

'Wasn't it Peter Warlock who said Vaughan Williams' music was all a bit too much like a cow looking over a gate?'

'An English cow looking over an English gate,' said Hester Banks. 'Rather nice, I've always thought.'

'Too patriotic for nowadays, I suppose,' said Edith mildly.

'I think one should be fond of the place one comes from, don't you?'

'I can't listen to my father's music dispassionately. Perhaps I will be able to one day. A lot of it was written for school choirs, so it had to be simple. It was a bit of luck when he got a commission. The Arthur sequence was meant to be for the Three Choirs Festival, I think.'

'Have you ever been to that?'

But the friendly inquiring face was edged out of vision by Johnny, now sweating considerably.

'What d'you think?' he said in a conspiratorial sort of way, leaning very close. 'What d'you think?'

'What about?'

'Her. What d'you think? Old Caroline.' He seemed full of glee.

'I didn't recognize her.'

'Older of course, we're all older. Not but what you manage to go on looking pretty good yourself, though I say it as shouldn't. But what a joke, what? I mean getting her here, first time for God knows how long. With you. I mean that's the thing, what? Getting her here with you.'

'Why?'

'You know. Cause of all the trouble, what?'

'What trouble?'

'You and me. Come on. We were married once, remember?' He bellowed with laughter. 'Don't say you've forgotten.'

'Of course I haven't forgotten. What is it to do with Caroline Cornish?'

'Cause of all the trouble.' He leant closer and whispered loudly in her ear, 'Adultery.'

Edith edged backwards and looked at him sternly.

'You didn't know?' he said, looking pleased but alarmed.

Edith looked round quickly, hoping they were not being overheard, and said, 'We fixed the divorce. You went to Brighton with an unknown woman. That was how it was done in those days.'

'You were being decent. Not dragging in Caroline.'

'But I thought we broke up when I got involved in all that council work.'

'Yes. Of course. And while you were at those meetings, there was I a couple of streets away, rogering Caroline Cornish.' He gave another bellow of laughter.

'So you were,' said Edith coldly. 'I'd forgotten.'

But she had never known. She pushed her way quite vigorously through the crowd, surprised by her own unregenerate rage.

'Food, food!' shouted Hermione, waving her arms, her shiny face suddenly quite close to Edith's.

'How wonderful,' said Edith with sudden sympathy, meaning not how wonderful but how horrible, to be married to

177

horrible Johnny. It was probably exposure to the elements, walking the dogs, rather than alcohol, that had given Hermione all those broken veins. 'What a wonderful party.'

'When we get to the cottage we won't have room for more than two people at a time. Rather a relief probably.'

'We should go through,' someone said. 'Hermione wants us to go through to the dining-room.'

'Are you coming to have some supper?' A rescuer. 'Allsop. My wife's a gardening friend of your brother's.'

'I used to be married to Johnny,' said Edith, 'and we've always got on quite well since the divorce, mainly because of our daughter, but just occasionally we madden each other all over again. I suppose you don't quite get over old hurts, unless you're a saint.'

'A saint's probably bristling with old hurts,' said Mr Allsop. 'I've always been thankful not to have been called upon to be one.'

They passed Alfred, who said, 'We're talking about Brontë.'

Alfred had seen at once that the whole thing was a nightmare, but not the worst sort. There were nightmares in which you knew there was another world, one to which, if you made a tremendous effort, you could return. Just before you hit the ground after the seemingly endless fall you could force yourself to wake up. There were other nightmares in which you knew you were out of reach, beyond the pull of gravity.

'They haven't abolished gravity, have they?' he said.

'Not as far as I know,' said Mrs Allsop. 'But as it's all mathematical, I can't understand it. It may be just as well not to know some of these things. I mean if we knew they'd abolished gravity, we'd all have to float about as if we were in a spaceship, wouldn't we? I don't think I can start that sort of thing at my time of life.'

'They oughtn't to have told us when they abolished God.'

'People do like to boast, though, don't they?'

178

Alfred liked Mrs Allsop. She had appeared one day to see whether he would open his garden to the public, and had agreed with him that the public would find it too unkempt, but he had been pleased that she had recognized the garden's merits, since he had kept it more or less as his mother had left it. Inside the house she had noticed the books, which had led to the discovery that they shared a liking for a certain long saga of sea stories, so that when Alfred mystified Edith by telling her that they were talking about Brontë, he was referring to the Sicilian estate which had been given to Nelson and recently sold by his descendants, and which Alfred had known and photographed, and their gossip had been gossip about Nelson and Emma Hamilton. This brief safe mooring could not last; moving obediently in the direction of the dining-room, he became separated from Mrs Allsop and found himself moving aside politely to allow a small dark-haired woman somewhat younger than himself to pass. She turned and smiled, and he remembered that she had been introduced to him as Laura Molesworth, or was it Lorna? Something about the eyebrows and the bridge of her nose had suddenly a piercing familiarity.

'You wouldn't have a brother called David?' he asked.

'I did have, yes. He died five years ago.'

'I'm sorry. He can't have been very old.'

'He had Aids.'

Alfred stood still. She looked at him coldly. 'Didn't you know he was a homosexual?'

'I hadn't seen him since we were children. I wish I'd known he was ill.'

'He wouldn't have wanted to see you. He only wanted to see what he called his family, the boyfriend and the boyfriend's boyfriends. It didn't include me.'

'Did they look after him?'

'Yes. Very well.'

She was not wearing a wedding ring. Her face was like an echo of his childhood friend's with all the vivacity wiped away; she was probably no more than fifty, but her dryness had a something final about it.

'I'm so sorry,' said Alfred.

She gave a small tight smile.

'I loved him,' said Alfred. 'We didn't know much about sex one way or the other in those days, but he was a very important part of my life.'

'He had that effect on people,' she said indifferently.

He had wanted to tell her; he owed it to Moley. She did not seem to want to continue the conversation.

Taking a plate, Alfred piled it with food from the dishes on the table. He found an empty window seat and sat down to eat the food, which was delicious. After this, he thought, we can go.

There was music, very loud. Young people appeared and began to dance vigorously, stamping their feet. One of them paused on his way to dance and told Edith he had taught for a few months in her school; he had enjoyed it, was still in touch with some of the people he had met, had taught in Ghana later but was now learning to be a solicitor; he had been staying with his parents for Christmas. He said hers was the only language school that took an interest in its students outside their classes; that was why they all enjoyed it so much. Edith responded gratefully, surprised as ever by praise and by her own need for it.

'Sporting of Johnny and Hermione,' said an oldish man with a handsome profile and very small rheumy eyes. 'Giving a huge party like this when they're bust. I'm not sure I would.'

'Some of those boys must be their sons. I wouldn't recognize them, though.'

'That's one, organizing the music there. Justin. Not much of a world for them to grow up in.'

'Oh, I don't know,' said Edith mildly. 'We had the Cold War. Don't you remember how we were all supposed to be living under the shadow of the bomb?'

This reply seemed to enrage her interlocutor; he became unexpectedly animated. 'We knew what was what. No one knows what's what these days. Everything's upside down. Topsy-turvy. Nothing sacred. No one cares for this country, we're a pathetic little third-rate power, our institutions are rotting from within, that's what they say, rotting from within. And who cares? What do they suggest we put in place of all these things they want to tear down? Monarchy? Parliament? The financial institutions? The Civil Service? Get rid of the Army, oh yes, can't afford it, can't defend ourselves, don't want to, that's the trouble, don't want to defend ourselves. Rather stay at home and rape old ladies.'

He paused to take a huge swig of red wine. Edith said, 'Perhaps we should all stop reading the newspapers.'

Successfully diverted, he began to inveigh against the press. Before Edith could make her escape Johnny reappeared, greeting her neighbour with a slap on the back which made him cough.

'Quite right, Hardy. She's fearfully left wing, you know.'

'All I say is, everything's gone to pot,' said Hardy, blowing his nose thunderously.

'There's probably some hope somewhere,' said Edith, standing up and beginning to move away. 'There usually is.'

'Where then?' he shouted after her.

'A new generation?' said Edith, gesturing towards the dancers.

He gave a sort of whoop, expressive of disbelief, but seemed to have cheered up.

'Women running the world?' she said, as a parting shot. 'European union?'

'Women and foreigners!' he shouted, now apparently in the best of good humour. 'Thank God I shan't live to see the day!'

Thank goodness Alfred was tall, Edith thought, seeing him across the room. She began to walk towards him. A woman

181

she had never seen before, with a large red face and a great deal of wiry white hair standing up round her head, said to her, 'Awful how old we are, isn't it?'

'I never think about age,' said Edith, almost truthfully.

'I think about it all the time,' said the woman. Her face had a noticeable droop to one side as if she might have had a slight stroke, but she looked quite healthy otherwise. 'I think how the future streams towards us like in cinema advertisements and then it becomes the present for a moment and then it rushes on into the past, and we battle against it trying to go the other way, clinging to our own little stories about ourselves as if we could keep them safe from the rush of rubble passing us. I mean all the debris of crashed empires and massive mistakes and we meantime trying to rebuild things and all the time just hurtling towards our private annihilations, dead or alive, gaga or gone. Flux, all flux.'

'That's not how I think at all,' said Edith firmly.

She turned away with some relief to greet Charles Warburton, who was not looking old at all but handsome and healthy in a plum-coloured smoking jacket and a white polo-necked shirt.

'We'll dance,' he said.

'The music's too loud.'

It was so loud he had not heard her. She followed him on to the dance floor among the stomping young people and the few alarmingly vigorous older couples and the pretty girls dancing apparently alone, apparently dreaming.

'Sleep-dancing,' said Edith, thinking of Sarah and beginning to move about with momentary mild euphoria in obedience to the beat.

'Brother?' Charles Warburton seemed to be saying. 'Insurance? Walls?'

She shook her head. Moving to rhythm – well, dancing, then – all she had ever wanted was someone to call the tune. Her father had done it so well, no one better – certainly not Charles Warburton – because of course she saw he was completely childish, grinning at her now quite amorously, talking about insurance and toy cars for grown-ups and the Cresta Run and the Eton and Harrow match of 1953.

'1953?' she said.

'My high spot,' he shouted. 'My peak performance. Nothing ever the same since.'

'A long time ago,' she said.

'Isn't it all?' he shouted. 'All the fun, all the glory, all the good times?'

'Certainly not,' she said indignantly.

He grabbed her by both arms. 'That's the spirit!' he cried. He strained her to his chest, which was quite hard and muscular, his clean manly smell not disagreeable at all. Nevertheless, she disengaged herself and taking his hand led him from the dance floor.

'Too noisy,' she said.

'We'll do this thing together,' he said, his arm round her shoulders. 'The off-road tracks, the jolly chaps being Mr Toad.'

'We won't, you know,' she said, putting a glass of wine into his hand. 'It's not really the sort of thing I want to do.'

'I don't believe you. You mean you don't want to come in on it? Don't want to be my partner?'

'I'm afraid not.'

'No vroom-vroom? No poop-poop up hill and down dale? You realize you're breaking my heart.'

'I'm so sorry.'

He looked at her sadly.

'I do believe you are,' he said.

Alfred was in a state of dissociation, leaning back on a sofa between two women who were talking to each other about people he did not know. From time to time one or other of them appealed to him for confirmation of some opinion or point of fact and he said, 'Absolutely,' which seemed to meet the case well enough.

He had noticed Edith dancing with Charles Warburton. It had made him smile; she looked so correct among the jostling, stomping crowd. At the same time her movements, though restrained, struck him as rather poetic. She waved her arms about like the child he remembered at dancing class pretending to be a tree, and gave from time to time a graceful turn, followed sometimes by a rather prosaic skip. She looked happy. Charles Warburton, opposite her, adopted a less appealing style, wriggling his hips and snapping his fingers. What an ass, Alfred thought. Surely Edith could not take him seriously? Alfred had decided, on thinking it over, to say nothing to her about Mrs Hurley's disclosures. He had telephoned Mrs Sainty, who had responded with her usual alacrity.

'I'll get on to it at once. I'd heard a rumour. I'll find out exactly what's going on and we'll get our protest letters in. If necessary, we'll call for a public inquiry.' She sounded quite pleased at the prospect. 'I'll call out the Home Guard,' she said.

Edith would go back to London and the scheme would be scotched in her absence. As usual where there was the possibility of a disagreement, they would have avoided confrontation. At the same time Alfred felt a certain sadness and, seeing Edith dancing now, he thought he wanted her to have what she wanted. We are getting older, he thought, becoming sentimental under the influence of the wine, she wants another game before bedtime. Perhaps if they defeated Charles Warburton's absurd scheme (and he had no doubt that they would, though it might take some time), the farmyard would revert to being of no interest to anyone and then after all Edith might buy it. It wouldn't be the end of the world to have a few students there sometimes. Not that he expected to like it, but perhaps he ought to put up with it for Edith's sake. But he would have to make it clear that he was not interested in Rose Brown. He could not undertake, in fact, ever to speak to Rose Brown.

'Don't you think it was too awful about the tape?' said the prettier of the two women on the sofa. 'I mean, who would do a thing like that?'

'Who indeed?' murmured Alfred.

The other woman, who had long hair and an uncertain smile, said, 'What tape?'

'He taped her in bed with George.'

'Good Lord, couldn't they get out?'

'What do you mean, get out?'

'Oh that sort of tape. I somehow imagined they were sort of roped up. Stupid of me. Taped, oh yes. Everybody tapes everything these days, don't they?'

'I wouldn't know how to, would you? I can't even manage the video. Anyway, I'm all on her side. Why shouldn't she have a last fling? She must be fifty if she's a day.'

'Yes, but everyone always gets so unpleasant about money. It's better not to know, I always think. Better not to tape. Think of having to listen to it. Besides, how did he know what they were doing?'

'Don't be silly, Belinda.'

'They might have been struggling with one of those king-size duvets,' said Belinda. 'Trying to put it into its cover.' She broke into wheezing giggles.

Alfred suddenly caught sight of Edith on the other side of the room.

'He thinks I'm silly too,' wheezed Belinda as he left.

'We've shot our bolt,' said Caroline Cornish, keeping a firm grip on her husband's arm and pushing determinedly through the crowd. 'Keep in touch.'

'Of course.' Edith looked sternly at Lord Inman, daring him to mention Derek; he gave a sickly smile and said, 'Rather.' It occurred to her that he might be slightly senile.

'I hope you've met some old chums,' said Hermione. Edith wondered if it was all right for her hands to be purple too, but thanked her warmly.

'We must go,' said Alfred as soon as she caught up with him.

'I've said goodbye. Have you?'

'I'll ring up in the morning,' said Alfred, leading the way across the room.

A perspiring girl with the face of an angel took Alfred by the arm and began to pull him towards the dance floor. He firmly disengaged himself and said, 'Sorry. Another time. My sister's going to be sick.'

Outside in the relentlessly clear air they had to scrape the frost from the windscreen. Edith took the driver's seat, on the assumption that Alfred would have had more to drink than she had.

'That was a very silly excuse,' she said. 'Anyone could see I wasn't going to be sick.'

'Sorry. It was a reversion to the past. Actually, the children's parties were even worse.'

'I was never sick.'

'Other people were. It would have been an acceptable excuse.'

Windscreen wipers going to clear the remains of the frost, they drove slowly down the drive between the still trees.

'You know Charles Warburton,' said Edith.

'Yes?'

'He has a plan for some kind of track for off-road racing. He wants to let them go all over his land and right up the valley, as far as I can make out.'

'That doesn't sound a very good idea.'

'No. You've still got a covenant on his farmyard, haven't you? So he couldn't get permission to use that for anything except farming, could he?'

'I doubt it.'

'Do you know anything about classifying byways?'

'A bit.'

'I think you ought to do something about it.'

'I will. Don't worry. I'll get in touch with Mrs Sainty, the guide-book lady, you know. She's an expert on planning. I'll ring her up tomorrow.'

'Good.'

Edith drove cautiously out on to the road. To her surprise the car then quite independently described a slow circle, ending up close to the hedge but facing in the right direction; however, it seemed to be stuck. Alfred got out to push, letting the car rock. At the fourth rock Edith was able to drive back on to the road.

'You'd better take over,' she said. 'I'm a coward.'

Alfred drove carefully, but even so they slithered all over the road. They sat in silence, tense with concentration. Edith had no wish to share with Alfred her retrospective anger with Johnny, nor did Alfred think of telling Edith about the death of Moley, whom she had hardly known. As they drove, the remorseless beauty of the frozen night induced in each of them a sense of detachment which eased, though it did not altogether assuage, their more intimate concerns.

They were about halfway home when a big hare emerged from the hedge and ran along the road just in front of them, seeming to keep pace with the car.

'Why do they do that?' asked Edith quietly.

'No one knows. Some people say they like the engine noise.'

'Perhaps they just like running.'

The hare sped easily on in front of them, obedient to its own laws.

'What do they do all day in winter?'

'Sit quite still in the grass.'

'And in the spring?'

'Dance.'

'Yes, I remember.'

After some time the hare swerved into a gateway and was gone, leaving the moonlit road mysteriously empty.

When they reached home, Edith said quietly as she got out of the car, 'I enjoyed that.'

Alfred, pausing to look at her over the roof of the car, said, 'You amaze me.'

'Not the party. The drive home.'

'Oh, yes. I enjoyed that, too.'

16

When Alfred woke, it was the hare that was in his mind, the moonlit road and the running hare; he and Edith sitting silently intent, the hare's world and their own momentarily at one, allowing them a sense of having received some kind of benediction. Underneath that picture was Moley's face as he had known it, and then a blank which was Moley's face as he lay dying. A different person of course, a man with a history unknown to Alfred, except in its first eleven years; but since Alfred could feel no change in himself since those times, only an accumulation of things seen and more or less useful knowledge acquired, he could only think of the Moley whose light had been extinguished as the same child whose light had been so bright. What right had he then himself to wake into such full awareness, such alert senses, such a fast, clear flow of consciousness? Then he remembered that sometimes a late night did have that effect, and got out of bed to stand at the window and watch the dawn. The sky was still clear, though drifts of mist filled the hollows in the direction of the ruined house and lurked milkily on the slope of the garden so that the smaller trees and shrubs showed only their frosty topmost branches; higher up, where the sun already touched the hillside, the trees cast long blue shadows over the frozen field. Alfred dressed quickly and, taking his camera, crept down the stairs and quietly let himself out of the front door; for once he did not want the dogs. He wanted a pristine world, whose patterns he might explore later in his darkroom.

He went round the side of the house furthest from the kitchen, so that the dogs would not hear him, and set off up the hill. As he climbed the fence into the wood at the top of the hill, a flock of long-tailed tits whispered in some tall thorn bushes. Beyond the wood the light was changing, the sky becoming an indeterminate soft grey. Two crows flew slowly through the silence. Alfred emerged from the trees to look down into the little valley, held motionless by the frost.

Edith woke furious. How could Hubert have let her marry Johnny? Anyone could have seen it was a mistake. But Hubert had not been there, he had been making his way in London, a clever young political journalist, not at all the sort of person she had known in those days. She got up quickly, let the dogs out, put the kettle on, laid two places for breakfast. She ought to have been relieved when Johnny had told her how badly he had behaved during their marriage. Hadn't she been feeling guilty that she hadn't treated him better herself? But she didn't feel relieved, she felt thoroughly affronted. When the telephone rang, she answered it abruptly, alarming Mrs Jupp, who was on the line and sufficiently apologetic already.

'I'm ever so sorry, it's the car, Sean can't do it, he's gone, he said he can't be late for John Jarrett, they're doing this job for someone to be finished by New Year, but he did say there's another car they might be able to swop for this when they've done it up, but we can't start it – this one I mean, it won't start.'

'I'll come,' said Edith.

On the way to the village she saw the squat, stooping figure of Lawrence Raven crossing the field towards the vicarage, muffled in scarves and topped by his absurd hat. A quick feeling of affection gave way to one of dissatisfaction. She had known Lawrence Raven all her life. How could she let the past, whose resonances had disturbed her sleep all week, make her no more than what she had done or failed to do? Her sympathy was with the future; all she wanted was to be part of it. Seeing Mrs Weeks re-adorned in her accustomed finery as she waited outside the cottage with Mrs Jupp was only a small consolation. Of course she was glad that between them she and Alfred had helped to prevent the collapse of Mrs Weeks's mysterious self-esteem, but she had hoped during her visit to achieve more than that. For the first time in her life she thought she might have to learn the virtues of resignation.

'There's a new plan.' It was Sarah at her breeziest.

'What is it?'

'I'm going to Hong Kong. I knew you'd be pleased. Robert's office fixed it all. I'm going to work for a PR firm out there – only part-time but not too bad pay. It's all because his boss thinks so highly of him. Isn't that good? Well, yes, he thinks highly of me too, of course. This firm is run by a friend of his. And the children will go to school there.'

'I'm so glad. I'm sure it's the right thing to do.'

'I can fight off the nubile secretaries, anyway. But the point is we want the children to come back every school holidays. I'll usually come with them of course, but it might just involve you sometimes. And Alfred too, but only if you would both positively like it, so you'll have to say. We both want them to know England's their proper home. You know Robert's parents were diplomats and he always minded that, and his sisters both married madmen. I don't know whether that had anything to do with it or not, really – no, they weren't foreign madmen, I don't think. Anyway, the thing is because it's only a part-time job, it would be sensible to save money by letting the house in London, but what do you think? What do you think Alfred would think? It would only be, well, I suppose about four months a year. We could do up the attics if he'd let us, and I think he quite likes the children, doesn't he? He was awfully nice to Alexander last time we came, explaining to him about woodlice and so on. Do you think you could ask him? But tactfully, Mum, I won't do it if he's at all doubtful, I know he likes being alone. Promise to tell me if he looks horrified. I mean I could pay rent or something or contribute or do the shopping. Promise to tell me truthfully what he thinks, promise.'

Edith stood at the bottom of the attic stairs and called for Alfred. There was no answer. She began to climb the steep steps. It was so long since she had been up there that she felt apprehensive, lest there should be some unsuspected secret, or else perhaps that the roof might be leaking. There were four attic bedrooms, quite large with dormer windows and three much smaller with one window each. The bathroom had become Alfred's darkroom. The lavatory, which was separate, had a small window looking out over the garden. She had locked herself in there once, in a temper, and watched Alfred and her mother weeding a rose bed, or rather her mother had been weeding and Alfred had been standing beside her. Now the lavatory door had a big photograph of an Indian holy man on it, and underneath that a smaller photograph of a herd of giraffes swinging their way at speed across a wide grassy plain, between sparse, stumpy trees. Edith had not realized to what an extent the photographs had taken over. They covered every available space and hung from every roof beam. She knew that Alfred, assisted by someone called Beryl, whom she had not met, was in the course of putting his old negatives and prints into better order so as to have an archive from which clients could ask for prints without his or Beryl's having to spend hours sorting through them, but she had had no idea of the extent of the collection. She supposed, now that she came to think of it, that that was foolish of her, since Alfred had been a photographer now for – what? – close on twenty-five years. So this was twenty-five years of looking. 'Just looking,' he used to say irritatingly as a boy when she asked him what he was doing, lanky and immobile under a tree or in the middle of a field. 'Just looking.'

Apart from the holy man and the giraffes, the landing at the top of the stairs reflected at random a world she knew.

Some of the prints were brown and faded, others looked more recent but had obviously been developed from old negatives. The garden in the evening, for instance, was better tended than it had been for years, and their mother was there, in conversation with a much younger John Jarrett, her profile outlined against his dark, ferocious features, and there was a back view of their father striding up the hill, a formidable bulk from behind, followed by the cairn, Pibroch, with his self-important air, and then there were their mother's hands held up towards the camera, cupped round a small frog. Edith opened a door (the beech trees at the top of the hill, clouds riding high over grass and stone walls), and found herself in a room full of places where she had never been, rock-strewn landscapes, huge spaces dwarfing groups of un-familiar trees, sea, a whole series of sea pictures, light on end-less waves beneath dark clouds, arrested waves adorned with scattered foam. In the next room there were beggars. Edith recoiled at first, but when she looked again they were after all not horrible but simply there: a woman beside a sleeping child, the child deformed; a scene on a railway station, where a well-dressed Indian couple waited, the father holding by the hand a little boy of five or six, clean and cared for, the parents looking away, embarrassed, the little boy gazing in wide-eyed curiosity at the creature hardly taller than himself approaching with a begging bowl on immense, swollen bare feet, feet bigger than those of any adult man, a comparatively normal child's face but with features blunted by some sort of idiocy, which had perhaps made the creature unaware of the full cruelty of its destiny. The picture showed the limpid curiosity of the undamaged child, and the well-meaning embarrassment of the parents, not knowing how to shield their darling from the world's sorrows. There were other cripples; a hundred years ago in England they would have been in peep shows at fairs or circuses. There were London street scenes, or perhaps it was Paris: rain on late-night streets, figures in doorways, white faces under dark-brimmed hats, a thin spiral of cigarette smoke against a shadowed wall – light on darkness or on lesser light, no more than that. And then another room, full of movement: people running, the hare again, caught in a blur of speed through clear, etched blades of grass, and Lydia, Lydia dancing, trailing white chiffon, Lydia's face pearly white, dark eyes, dark, floating hair (surely Lydia had not had hair as black as that? But you could do anything with a camera, Edith supposed), Lydia leaping a fence, Lydia jumping high in the air, laughing, Lydia who had jumped like that from a cliff – had she been laughing then? – and there were the cliffs, with turbulent seas below them, and fulmars flying and kittiwakes perched on narrow ledges, and gannets plunging through the air in tremendous dives.

The biggest room was full of crowds, markets, bazaars. Morocco, perhaps; Indian crowds covering some immense concourse, in Delhi, Edith thought, a funeral procession; a different brightness on an Italian or a Spanish square, a short man in a dark suit making a speech; a huge quarry full of men with pick-axes; then an apparent army of street-sweepers; and everywhere such crowds, the light coming from the side and usually low, an evening or an early morning light. Perhaps that was why the pictures implied no judgements, Edith thought. Perhaps the people, incidents, objects, mountains, trees, were incidental, and the camera's only love affair was with the light. The world was light, through which people and objects moved in some impenetrable measure. Even the landscapes had often a slight insubstantiality, as if the light might have trembled for a moment. The crowds so lit had seldom an obvious reason for their having gathered. Sometimes they looked like defeated armies, sometimes like a multitude coming together praising God. Praise was certainly there, as if the consciousness behind the camera had had only one reaction to beauty and ugliness, joy, pain, error, tragedy: simply praise. This had been Alfred's life, Edith thought, moved; day after day his solitary cry of praise had risen into

the indifferent air. His vision was not hers; but she understood
its fierce coherence. Making her way back towards the stairs,
she was confronted again by the cupped hands of her mother.
There was an ink mark on one finger; the fingers were long,
square-tipped, curled to contain the frog. Turning away, she
saw the ditch at the top of the hill, frozen grasses and weeds,
a rivulet of shining water.

Alfred found Edith sitting at the bottom of the attic stairs.
She said she felt she had been inside his head.

'How was it?' he asked.

'I wish you had been a painter or a poet. You would have
been famous, I know.'

'You're the famous one.'

'I did want to be, once. I suppose it is a vulgar ambition.'

'You wanted to do good and useful things, that isn't
vulgar.'

'You never cared about success, even when you were
supposed to be a fashion idol. Perhaps you despised our father
for wanting it so much.'

'I was never a fashion idol. What an odd idea. I was just
tagging along after Augustine and Lydia because I liked the
stir they made.'

'I have always taken myself too seriously, that's my
trouble.'

'No one could doubt that you are a serious person, Edith.'

'Don't laugh at me. You are an artist, and that is rare, so
you should share your vision. But there we are, we could
argue for ever. Now, listen. Sarah has had a change of plan.
But we must go downstairs to discuss it. She says I must
watch you carefully to see what your true reaction is.'

The day Edith left to go back to London was the day the
thaw began. She drove through wet mist to the motorway,
where lorries thundered past her, scattering spray and slowing
her progress. She was looking forward to getting back to
London. Whenever she arrived there, she felt her spirits rise.

Hermione had said to her, 'Poor you, living in London. I hate it more and more whenever I go. So crowded and so filthy and everyone's black.' Edith had answered mildly, 'I like it,' but what she really meant was that she couldn't bear to live anywhere else, that London was life and interest and her own square and the tall trees in its garden where the blackbird sang late on summer evenings. In fact, if the weather was going to improve she might ask a few people to dinner, just two or three at a time so they could talk; if Hubert was in a good mood, he might feel like doing the cooking. But first she would have to see that everything was in order for the new year's language courses, jolly up the staff and put the timetables right because they would be sure to have muddled them. And then Sarah might need help to get the house let and herself and the children off to Hong Kong – she was not leaving her job for a few weeks and would be short of time. Robert was leaving almost immediately. Edith liked doing things with Sarah because Sarah was so brisk and efficient; if the two of them put their minds to something, they could achieve wonders in a week or two.

'Nymphs and shepherds come away,' she sang. She wondered if schoolgirls sang that sort of song any more. Probably not – the correct little English voices she remembered would sound old-fashioned now. 'Kookaburra sits on the old gum tree-ee' – you could sing that in an Australian accent – 'Merry, merry king of the bush is he-e' – but it was unconvincing; she had never been any good at accents, and that, if anything, was South African. 'Where e'er you walk' – her first solo at a school concert – 'Trees where you walk shall bend, shall bend, into-o a shade' – her father looking as embarrassed as she was, although they both knew she did sing well. But it had been her mother she had dreamt about last night, arriving at a hotel. Reception is round the corner they had said, and she had said, 'My mother is tired, we can't wait,' but her mother was amused, not being tired at all, and they had to step on to a boat and set off on a journey. She had had this dream many times and forgotten it, and then at odd moments it would come into her waking mind, the two of them setting off on a journey on quite a big boat, a ferry of some sort. They must not miss it, but they did not expect to miss it, they were not unduly anxious, travelling together quite companionably. So what did that mean, if anything? She did not know, but was glad they were at peace together. She hoped it was not a dream about death because she did not want to die. 'Jack be nimble, Jack be quick, Jack jump over the candlestick.' She beat time on the steering-wheel, accelerating to pass a lorry.

She would catch up on the political gossip when she saw Hubert; she had never lost her interest in that game. It was a pity Sarah wasn't interested in politics, she'd be so good at it, and she was so much better qualified, with her university degree and her successful career, but it was impossible to imagine. Perhaps she might become a Euro-MP, the pay was good. In due course, and if the new arrangement was a success, and if Charles Warburton's schemes were defeated, Sarah and Robert might buy the farm buildings and convert them into a holiday house for themselves. Alfred would like the idea, she was sure of it, just as she was sure he had been genuinely pleased when she had told him about Sarah's change of plan. Alfred had his own methods and his own mode of being; she understood that better now and she was not going to mention Rose Brown to him again. But it would be nice for him to have the children there. She must ask Hubert how much one did earn as a Euro-MP. It might be quite interesting. She wondered if she should think of it herself – was one too old at sixty? She'd heard they were quite short of candidates. She would just ring up this Beryl person and see that she did not throw away too many of those extraordinary photographs, there would be no need to mention it to Alfred.

She parked her car in her usual space, pleased to find it empty, and looked up at the windows of her first-floor flat. There was a light on in one of the rooms. She wondered whether Sarah had been round and left a light on to deter burglars; she was the only person apart from Edith herself who had a key, since one of the small and slightly inconvenient conventions which she and Hubert observed was that neither had a key to the other's flat. She climbed the stairs quietly, listening for suspicious sounds, and opened the door, saying tentatively, 'Sarah?' There was a smell of spices, lemon grass, coriander. How right the green sofa looked, just there.

'I borrowed Sarah's key,' said Hubert, looking anxious, wearing a striped cooking apron, his face pink and well-shaved.

'You've cooked something. How lovely.' Edith put down her suitcase.

'Wait,' he said, holding up his hand. 'This is important.'

She stood still. She thought, If he leaves me I'll die.

'I've completely given up smoking,' he said.

'I see,' said Edith seriously.

'Do you? Do you see, Edith?'

'Yes. I do see. And I am so glad, dear Hubert.'

Alfred wondered whether they ought to have kept the piano; one of Sarah's children might have liked it. The girl Catherine was always dancing. She had a particularly repetitive routine in which she took a few steps to one side and then a few to the other, swinging her arms and chanting monotonously. It had been a relief when she had given up demanding an audience, but he supposed it might be said that at four years old she showed at least a sense of rhythm. But the piano had gone. When Alfred was away so much and there was no one to see that it was tuned, he had agreed with Edith that they should sell it. It was a good upright Broadwood and they had got a reasonable price for it, but in any case the fact was that neither of them had liked to see it there, with the swivel chair in front of it from which their father could turn from desk to piano and back again when he was composing and on which he had sat so often playing to their mother as she waited weakly in her chair to die, dozing a little, drugged against the pain, always waking when he finished a piece to say she'd liked it.

Alfred was out in the garden; the field was difficult to walk on now that the thaw had started because only the top layer of soil had thawed, and underneath that the ground was still frozen solid, so that it was like walking on seaweed-covered rocks. But the smell was good, almost of spring, and Alfred breathed deeply, feeling as usual when returned to solitude as if he were physically expanding to fill the waiting space. The dogs on the other hand enjoyed company, even Edith's although she did not much like them and pushed them off the chairs; they followed him towards the farm buildings in a damp and disheartened bunch until the terrier spotted a squirrel which had been roused by the thaw to forage for food and set off in a series of excited jumps to pursue it. The others followed. Alfred, relieved that they were exercising themselves since he had no intention of taking them for a walk in such weather, followed them only as far as the corner of the field beyond the farm buildings where the ground was humped and irregular around what remained of the founda-tions of the house which had once stood there, irregularities so slight that if you had not known there had been a house there you might have thought it was just what was known locally as gruffy ground, the upheaval left by the activities of the lead miners since Roman and perhaps prehistoric times. The Barwell family who had lived in the house had surfaced for a hundred years or so and disappeared more or less without trace. The farmhouse which they must have passed every day and which they had considered too modest for their needs had long preceded and long outlasted them, solid and plain and satisfying with its sash windows and the shell-shaped hood over the front door. Into it not so long ago had come Arthur Ashby, of local stock, son of a shoemaker, possessor of an unheralded talent, tormented by that talent, which had taken him up in the social scale and brought him a wife whose virtues he adored without perhaps understanding them, but which would not let him rest, making him shout, 'Rejoice, rejoice,' and despise his son who could not sing in tune. But he had left the son the house.

Walking back towards it, Alfred found himself looking at the house critically, because he was thinking of it in relation to Sarah and the children. It struck him that though he had thought much about its past he could not remember ever before having thought about its future. He had kept it sound, he thought, repaired the roof. He had maintained the garden, so that even now Mrs Allsop could recognize his mother's touch. He had resisted the madman who had wanted to build a ski-slope in the valley just as he would with his allies resist the new madman who wanted to turn the place into a noisy race-track. The children would know it all as it was meant to be known. Already that morning he had telephoned Lawrence for the name of the man who had recently done some work at the vicarage, with a view to the repainting of the attics. He had spoken to Beryl too, and told her they must get on with clearing out the photographs. 'We can throw most of them away,' he had said. All the wandering he had done had not taken him away from the house in any fundamental sense; it was him, he it, they took their place where their place was, together, shouldering their past. I have not denied my inheritance, he thought. For what that is worth.